JESS THE BORDER COLLIE
The Sacrifice

Jenny crept across the yard, her eyes on the window. The tree was set slightly back so that she could see inside the living-room. A fire burned brightly in the grate and Fiona was sitting on the hearth-rug with a book in her lap. There was a smile on her lips and she seemed to be speaking softly to someone. Jenny edged closer still and caught her breath. Jess was lying curled up on the rug beside Fiona, looking up at her.

Suddenly, the Border collie's ears pricked and he looked towards the window. Then, seeing Jenny there, he rose and quietly trotted over. Jenny's eyes pricked with tears as she looked at him through the glass. For a long moment Jess just stayed there, his eyes fixed on hers. He put his head to one side and laid it against the window. Jenny stretched out a hand, then drew it back quickly and stood out of view as she heard a faint voice from inside the room. Fiona was calling to Jess. He gave Jenny one last look then turned and ran back to Fiona.

THE SACRIFICE

LUCY DANIELS

ILLUSTRATED BY SHEILA RATCLIFFE

*Hodder
Children's
Books*

a division of Hodder Headline plc

Special thanks to Helen Magee

Text copyright © 1999 Ben M. Baglio
Created by Ben M. Baglio, London W12 7QY
Illustrations copyright © 1999 Sheila Ratcliffe

First published in Great Britain in 1999
by Hodder Children's Books

A Catalogue record for this book is available from the British Library

ISBN 0 340 73596 1

Typeset by Avon Dataset Ltd, Bidford-on-Avon, Warks

Printed and bound in Great Britain by
The Guernsey Press Co. Ltd, Channel Islands

Hodder Children's Books
a division of Hodder Headline plc
338 Euston Road
London NW1 3BH

1

'So *that's* Thistle Cottage,' said Jenny Miles. She looked doubtfully at the little whitewashed house at the end of the muddy track, then at her father, Fraser Miles. 'It isn't very big, is it?'

It was Jenny's first look at the cottage that was to be their home for the next few weeks. Jess, Jenny's black-and-white Border collie, ran ahead and scrabbled at the cottage door.

'Jess looks as if he wants to explore,' Ellen

Grace said, encouragingly.

'Why don't you catch him up?' Fraser said, reaching in his pocket and giving Jenny the key.

Jenny ran after Jess. The wind blew her shoulder-length fair hair across her face. It was the beginning of December and the track beneath her feet was already rutted with frozen mud. She opened the door of the cottage and Jess disappeared at once, racing through the rooms.

'There are only two bedrooms,' Fraser said, as he reached the door. 'It'll be a bit of a squeeze when you're back from college, Matt.'

'Oh, I'll be all right sleeping on the sofa,' Jenny's brother Matt said, poking his head round the door.

Thistle Cottage belonged to the McLays. They had offered it to the Mileses to help make amends while their farmhouse, Windy Hill, was being repaired. It had been severely damaged by a fire, accidentally started by Fiona, Anna and Calum McLay's daughter.

Jenny followed her father into the kitchen. 'It must be funny coming back here, Mrs Grace,' Jenny said, as she looked round the tiny room. Ellen Grace had once rented Thistle Cottage from Calum McLay but because of a long-standing grudge against Fraser, he had evicted her out of spite when she came to work for the Mileses. It seemed very bare and basic compared to the big cluttered kitchen at Windy Hill. There was an ordinary cooker instead of the Aga Jenny was used to and the kitchen table was a small plastic-topped one, not at all like the huge wooden table in the farmhouse kitchen. But the walls were painted bright sunshine yellow and they looked cheerful even on a dull December day.

'It's a nice little cottage,' Ellen Grace said. 'I decorated it only last year. I hope you like the colours.'

'It's very cheerful,' Jenny said, smiling at Mrs Grace.

'It's just as well you'll be away at college during the week, Matt,' Fraser Miles said to him, peering into the sitting-room. 'But if you find it too uncomfortable, I can manage on my own most weekends.'

'No way,' said Matt firmly. 'You know I love helping out with the sheep, Dad, and you're going to have to start scanning the ewes soon to see how many are pregnant. You can't manage that on your own.'

Matt was nineteen and away at college, studying agriculture. He came home as often as he could to help with the work at the Mileses' sheep farm.

Jenny's father kept a thousand Scottish Blackface sheep with the help of only a couple of farmhands.

'OK,' Fraser gave in. 'If you're offering to help, I'm not going to refuse!'

'Good!' Matt said with a grin.

'What do you think of Thistle Cottage, Jess?' Jenny said as the Border collie came running into the kitchen. She bent down and gave him a cuddle. Jess wagged his tail and looked up at her, his head tilted to one side. 'There isn't very much to explore, is there?' she said, smiling.

The sheepdog sat down at Jenny's feet and gazed at her adoringly. He'd been born with a badly twisted leg which meant he would never make a working dog. Jenny had persuaded her father to let her keep the little puppy as a pet and to have his leg operated on. Now Jess was as good as new and the two of them were inseparable. No matter what happened to Jenny, as long as she had Jess by her side she was happy!

'He'd be quite content to live anywhere so long as you were there, Jenny.' Mrs Grace laughed, her warm blue eyes smiling at Jenny. 'Come on, I'll show you the other rooms.'

Ellen Grace had come to Windy Hill as

housekeeper some months after Jenny's mother had been killed in a riding accident. At first, Jenny had been wary of having someone take her mother's place but Mrs Grace had never tried to do that and now Jenny thought of her as one of the family.

Besides the kitchen, there was a small sitting-room, a bathroom and two tiny bedrooms. The sitting-room had a sofa and two armchairs, a drop-leaf table and a sideboard against the wall.

'Oh, this looks cosy!' Jenny exclaimed, as she took in the fresh white walls and rose-coloured curtains. She was even more delighted with her little bedroom. It had blue-patterned wallpaper and white paintwork and there was a striped blue and white blind at the window.

She turned to the housekeeper. 'I think you're a great interior decorator,' she said.

Mrs Grace laughed. 'I don't know about that,' she said. 'It's all very simple.'

'It's lovely,' Jenny insisted. 'It's just a pity you can't be here with us.'

Mrs Grace nodded. 'I know,' she said. 'But I'll come over every morning and evening to see to the cooking and housework.' As there wasn't enough room for the Mileses *and* Ellen Grace all to stay at Thistle Cottage, the housekeeper was going to help out Anna McLay and sleep at Dunraven until the repairs to Windy Hill were complete.

'What about Jess?' Jenny said.

'I thought I'd take him with me to Dunraven,' Mrs Grace replied. 'Rather than leaving him on his own while you're at school.'

'That's a good idea, isn't it, Jess? You'll have Toby to play with,' Jenny said, rubbing Jess's ears. 'You and Toby are great friends.' Toby was a Border terrier. He belonged to young Paul McLay, the McLays' eight-year-old son.

'OK,' said Fraser Miles, putting his head round the bedroom door. 'Let's get moving. I want to look in on Windy Hill. The builder should have arrived by now to start the repairs.'

Jenny's heart sank as her father turned his jeep into the farmyard at Windy Hill. She still hadn't got used to the state their home was in, although it was more than a month now since the fire. The old stone farmhouse stood desolate and empty, its red roof scorched and sagging in places. The entire upstairs floor was badly water-damaged and Jenny's bedroom – which had been gutted by the fire – had boarded-up windows. The paintwork was peeling where it had been burned and the walls were blackened by smoke. It was such a sorry sight it made Jenny want to cry. The stables had survived and Fraser Miles was still able to use them but the new lambing barn that he had built with the profits of the previous year's lambing had been burned to the ground. The builders had cleared away the remains but Jenny felt a lump in her throat as she remembered how proud her father had been of his new barn.

There was a white van already parked in the yard and a grey-haired man in a waxed jacket was standing with a clipboard in his hand, looking up at the gable wall of the farmhouse. He turned as Mr Miles drew to a halt and began to walk towards them.

'That's Joe Thorburn, the builder,' Matt said, as Fraser leaped out of the driver's seat and went to meet him.

Jenny, Matt and Mrs Grace followed.

'I've got a fair idea of the repairs that need to be done,' Mr Thorburn said, as he and Fraser shook hands. 'We'll start on the house this afternoon. I guess that's the most important thing. We'll do the roof first, then I'll get some of the men working on the new barn and the rest can concentrate on the inside of the house.'

Fraser Miles nodded. 'The sooner we can move back in the better,' he said. 'How long do you think it'll take?'

Joe Thorburn looked at the sky. 'That depends on the weather,' he said. 'Let's see. If we can work right through then we should get finished by the end of January, but if we get really heavy snow that's going to hold things up. We could be talking well into February.'

'February!' Jenny protested. 'But that's *ages* away.'

Joe shook his head. 'You can't argue with the weather, lass,' he said. 'Let's just hope the snow holds off until we get the outside work done. If things get really bad it could be March before we get the house habitable. But I promise you we'll work as quickly as we can.'

Jenny looked up. The sky was heavy with clouds but they weren't snow clouds – not yet. Windy Hill was on the border between Scotland and England, its fields to the east stretching to the cliffs that ran along the coast. She shivered as a sudden wind blew a chill off the sea. Winters in the Borders could be harsh.

'Just do the best you can, Joe,' Fraser said, his eyes

serious. He turned as a car drew into the farmyard.

'There's Miss Stewart,' Ellen Grace said, as a woman with short dark hair got out of a car that had just pulled into the yard.

Marion Stewart was the insurance representative from the company that had insured Windy Hill. According to Carrie Turner, Jenny's best friend, Miss Stewart had taken a shine to Fraser Miles – and Jenny wasn't at all sure she liked that idea.

Marion Stewart walked across the yard, her eyes on Fraser. She smiled as she approached and laid her hand on his arm. 'I hoped I'd find you here, Fraser,' she said. 'I take it everything is going smoothly?'

Mr Miles ran a hand through his hair. 'It's a bit early to say, Marion,' he told her. Then he added, 'I hope you haven't brought any bad news.'

Marion shook her head. 'Not at all,' she assured him. 'I came to agree some estimates with Joe.'

'That's all right then,' Fraser said. 'I'll leave you to it. We've got to move house this afternoon.'

Marion swung round as Fraser and the others made to leave. 'I'd be delighted to help you,' she offered.

Fraser smiled as he looked at Marion Fraser's smart blue suit, then shifted his gaze to Matt, Jenny and Ellen. They were all wearing jeans. 'Thanks for the offer,' he said, 'but you'd probably spoil your clothes.'

Jenny cast a look behind her as they went. Marion Stewart was watching them go. She looked disappointed. Jenny began to think that perhaps Carrie was right about Miss Stewart.

Carrie rushed out of the house to meet them as they drove into Cliffbay, the nearby fishing village where the Turners lived. The Mileses had been staying with them since the fire. Cliff House was down by the harbour, a big stone house facing the sea. Carrie's mother, Pam, was an artist and Gordon, her father, ran boat trips to Puffin Island, a nature reserve just off the coast.

'What's the cottage like?' Carrie asked breathlessly, her bright red hair streaming out behind her as she ran towards them.

'Small,' said Jenny. 'But Mrs Grace has done it up really nicely.'

Carrie bent to pat Jess. The Border collie leaped up, enjoying the fuss Carrie made of him. 'What about your room?'

'For goodness sake, Carrie, let them get inside

before you bombard them with questions,' her mother said, laughing, as she too came to greet them. Pam Turner, like Carrie, had red hair, but hers was cut short. 'Come and have some lunch before you pack up.'

Jenny and the others followed Mrs Turner into Cliff House while Carrie continued her barrage of questions.

'I knew it,' she said, grinning, when Jenny told her about Marion Stewart. 'I reckon she's after your dad.'

Jenny looked at her father as he sat down at the big kitchen table. 'I think Dad's got too much on his mind to be bothered with Miss Stewart,' she said, looking at her father's face. He was smiling and chatting but Jenny could see the shadow of worry behind his eyes.

'I'm starving,' Matt said as he sat down.

'So what else is new?' Mrs Grace joked and everyone laughed.

'I wish our relatives from Australia weren't coming so soon and that you could stay on at Cliff House,' Carrie confessed to Jenny.

'You can come and visit at Thistle Cottage,' Jenny said. 'And we'll see each other all the time at school.'

'Only two weeks till the Christmas holidays,'

Carrie said. 'I wonder how Ian will enjoy Christmas in Canada. He was so lucky getting off school early.' Ian Amery was Mrs Grace's nephew. He had chosen to live in Scotland with Mrs Grace, but had gone to Canada to spend the Christmas holiday with his parents.

'He says he's going to learn to ski and then teach us when he gets back – if there's any snow,' Jenny told Carrie.

Carrie snorted. 'Of course there'll be snow!' she said. 'That would be great fun.'

But Jenny wasn't so sure about how great a long, hard winter would be. Snow wouldn't be good for the sheep *or* the building work at Windy Hill.

'That's the last of the boxes,' Carrie said, as she heaved a carton into the back of the jeep. She looked at what was left of the Mileses possessions. 'There isn't much, is there? Honestly, Jenny, don't you feel really angry with Fiona?'

Jenny sighed. Fiona McLay had accidentally started the fire in Jenny's bedroom on Bonfire Night when she had been snooping around Windy Hill. Very little belonging to Jenny had survived the fire. Luckily the possession that Jenny valued the most

had been salvaged – a photograph of her mother.

'Of course I'm angry,' she said to Carrie. 'But Fiona made herself really ill with worry about what she did.'

Carrie shook her hair back from her face. 'That doesn't make it all right,' she said fiercely. 'Fiona has always hated you. I bet she hasn't changed.'

Carrie was right. Fiona McLay had always picked on Jenny, laughing at her for not being interested in fashionable clothes. She had called Jess names too, saying he was Jenny's 'lame dog'. And her father, Calum McLay, was just as bad. He had been trying for years to make Fraser Miles sell Windy Hill to him because he wanted to plant trees on the land.

'Time to go home, Jenny,' Mrs Grace said, as she came out of the house.

Jenny looked at her, suddenly miserable. 'Thistle Cottage isn't home,' she said. 'Only one place is home – Windy Hill.'

Ellen Grace laid a hand on her arm. 'We'll all live there again, Jenny,' she said. 'You'll see.'

Jenny reached her hand into the box Carrie had just loaded. She lifted the framed photograph of her mother out and gazed at it. The photograph had been taken when her mother had been eleven years old and Jenny was always amazed at how like her mother she looked.

Jenny sighed and a warm tongue licked her hand. She looked down as Jess put his head on one side and looked up at her appealingly.

'Oh, I miss Windy Hill so much, Jess,' she said. 'When are we going to be able to go back there?'

Jess licked her hand again and made a soft snuffling sound in his throat. Jenny smiled and bent to give him a hug. 'No matter what happens, I'll always have you,' she whispered. 'No one will ever take you away from me.'

2

It seemed strange to Jenny to return to Thistle Cottage the next day after school instead of going home with Carrie. The school bus dropped her off at Dunraven and Jenny hurried down the track to the little cottage, eager to see Jess.

Jess hurled himself at Jenny, almost knocking her over. He was nearly a year old now, no longer a puppy, but with his four white socks and white chest he still looked adorable.

'How did Jess get on at Dunraven, Mrs Grace?' she asked, as she dumped her schoolbag on the kitchen floor.

'He and Toby had a great time together,' Mrs Grace assured her, as Jenny hugged Jess.

'Is Fiona all right with him?' Jenny persisted. 'She's never liked him. She even threw a stick at him once.'

'Oh, Fiona didn't take any notice of him,' Mrs Grace replied, frowning. 'In fact she hardly came out of her room all day. She's very ill and depressed, Jenny. Anna McLay is afraid she's heading for a nervous breakdown.'

'She must feel so guilty about what she did,' Jenny said seriously. Then she smiled as Jess butted her. 'I'm glad you had a good time with Toby, Jess,' she said.

Mrs Grace was stirring a dark mixture in a big bowl. Jenny dipped a finger in the bowl and tasted the mixture. 'Christmas pudding,' she said. 'It tastes great.'

'It'll taste even better when it's cooked,' Mrs Grace laughed. She handed Jenny a wooden spoon. 'Here, make a wish.'

Jenny stirred the mixture in the bowl and closed her eyes. She had only one wish – to get back to

Windy Hill as soon as possible.

'Your turn,' Jenny said, giving the spoon back.

The housekeeper opened her eyes. 'I've wished,' she said.

'What did you wish for?' Jenny said when she noticed how worried Mrs Grace looked.

Mrs Grace sighed. 'For Fiona to get better,' she said. 'Her mum says she hardly ever speaks to anybody and she bursts into tears if Anna mentions inviting somebody to visit.'

Jenny hated to see Mrs Grace worried. She was usually so cheerful. 'Is there anything I can do?' she asked.

Mrs Grace shook her head. 'I don't think there's anything anyone can do, Jenny,' she said. 'All I know is that Anna is at her wits' end.' The housekeeper looked at Jenny and Jess and her frown softened. 'Anyway, it's good to see you two so happy,' she said. 'Dunraven is such an unhappy house at the moment.'

Jenny gave Jess another cuddle. Thistle Cottage wasn't ideal but at least she had Jess. 'Jess always helps me when I feel sad,' she said.

'You're lucky,' Mrs Grace replied. 'I don't think anyone can help Fiona at the moment.'

★ ★ ★

However, a few days later Mrs Grace told Jenny that Fiona seemed to be making some progress.

'At first she wouldn't come out of her room at all when I was there,' the housekeeper said on Wednesday. 'But today she was sitting in the living-room when I arrived and instead of rushing off to her room, she stayed for a little while. She seemed to be watching Jess.'

Jenny felt an immediate alarm. 'She didn't do anything to him, did she?'

Ellen Grace looked shocked. 'No, Jenny, she just watched him. It's odd. She doesn't bother with Toby but she seems to like Jess.'

Jenny didn't say anything. She couldn't believe that Fiona could have changed her attitude towards Jess.

When she told Carrie what Mrs Grace had said, Carrie agreed. 'Huh!' she scoffed next day at school. 'Fiona will never change. She's always made fun of Jess. Just you tell Mrs Grace to watch out for her. I wouldn't trust Fiona McLay with *my* dog.'

Jenny sighed. 'Maybe we should feel sorry for her,' she said. 'After all, she must be lonely up at Dunraven with no one her own age to talk to.'

Carrie looked at Jenny in amazement. 'How can you even *think* of feeling sorry for her after what she did to you?' she asked. 'Fiona was perfectly happy to let you take the blame for the fire at Windy Hill.'

Jenny sighed again. What Carrie said was true. Fiona *had* let everyone believe that Jenny had caused the fire by leaving a candle lit in her bedroom. She'd even spread rumours at school that the fire was Jenny's fault.

'Forget Fiona,' Carrie advised. 'It'll be Christmas soon and there's lots of things to look forward to.'

On the last day of term, Jenny rushed in from school full of news about the class Christmas party.

'We had mince pies and cake and a disco in the school hall,' she told Mrs Grace, as Jess launched himself at her in welcome. She plonked herself down at the little kitchen table and Jess put his head in her lap. 'Thank goodness it's the school holidays. Now I can have you with me all the time,' she said, looking down at the Border collie. Jess's tail thumped happily on the floor.

'How's Fiona?' Jenny asked.

Mrs Grace smiled. 'A little better, I think,' she

replied. 'You know, I'm certain she looks forward to seeing Jess every day. She certainly seems to perk up when he arrives.'

'That's good,' Jenny agreed.

Then Jenny noticed that Mrs Grace was frowning. 'What's wrong?' she asked. 'If Jess is helping Fiona you should be glad.'

'Of course I am, Jenny,' Mrs Grace assured her. 'That isn't what I'm worried about.'

'What then?' asked Jenny.

Mrs Grace shrugged. 'I'm just wondering how Fiona will get on without Jess,' she said. 'As you said, Jenny, now that you're on holiday Jess won't be going to Dunraven for a while. I think Fiona will really miss him.'

Jenny frowned. She was pleased that Jess was being a help, but a part of her resented the time Fiona spent with Jess – and she was still a little suspicious of Fiona's new attitude to him. She couldn't help feeling that Fiona was up to something.

Mrs Grace didn't mention the subject of Fiona and Jess again until a few days later. It was three days before Christmas. As Jenny was going to spend the morning at Windy Hill with her father and Matt, who was home for the Christmas holidays, Mrs Grace asked if she could take Jess to Dunraven with her. Reluctantly, Jenny agreed.

'Thank you, Jenny. I think Fiona will be very glad to see him,' Mrs Grace said as she left. 'We'll be back just after lunch. See you then.'

Jenny waved goodbye as Mrs Grace and Jess set off up the track to Dunraven; then her father called her and she swung round. She was really looking forward to seeing how the work was going on – and she was going to help scan the pregnant ewes!

Jenny looked anxiously at the farmhouse as they turned into the yard; it was a hive of activity and noise. There were ladders propped against the walls and a pile of wooden beams stacked in a corner under a tarpaulin cover. A lorry stood at the far end of the farmyard and two men were unloading bags of cement from it. Two others were operating a cement mixer. The builders had done some work to the stables so that Fraser could use them for penning ewes but it was the work on the house that most interested Jenny.

'It looks so strange,' she said to Matt, gazing up at the roof of the farmhouse. The roof was stripped down to the beams. It no longer looked like their old house.

'They're having to replace some of the rafters before tiling it,' Matt told Jenny.

The downstairs windows still had glass in them but most of the upstairs ones were boarded up and there was a growing pile of rubble in the yard in front of the house.

'How does Joe think it's going, Dad?' Matt asked.

'Pretty well,' said Fraser. 'The weather has been good so far and, once they get the roof done, they can start on the inside. Joe intends to drop by later. But meantime, we have the ewes to scan.' He turned as a van drew into the yard. 'Here's Tim Dobson now.'

Fraser Miles had hired Mr Dobson to come to the farm and scan the pregnant ewes to see how many lambs they could expect. He was a young man, only a few years out of agricultural college, with fair hair. Matt and Jenny helped to herd the ewes from the lower field into the holding pens in the farmyard while Tim and Fraser set up the equipment. Jake and Nell, Fraser Miles's two working sheepdogs, wove in and out of the flock, guiding them towards the pens. There were more pens set up in the stables so that the ewes could be divided after scanning. The dogs were used to this work but Jenny always admired how quickly they could separate the ewes, herding them into pens at Matt's command.

'Jess would be good at this,' Jenny said, as she closed the door of the last pen and bent to give Jake's ears a rub. Jake and Nell were Jess's parents.

Jenny watched as Mr Dobson and her father checked the scanning machine in the stables. There was a box with a waterproof cover and inside it was a monitor with several control knobs below it.

'You'll be able to see the unborn lambs on the screen, Jenny,' Fraser Miles said. He turned to Matt. 'Let's get going then, son.'

Jenny stood beside Tim as he plugged in the probe that would scan the ewes. It fitted into the front of the monitor. He twiddled a knob, and nodded at Fraser. 'Ready.'

Fraser and Matt brought out the first ewe, turning her on her back while Mr Dobson passed the probe over the animal's belly. 'Look at the screen,' he said to Jenny.

Jenny looked. 'I can't see anything,' she said,

frowning. 'Just fuzzy lines.'

Tim Dobson reached across and pointed with his free hand. 'There,' he said. 'Look! Can't you see something moving?' His finger traced the outline of the image on the screen. Jenny looked closely at the monitor and suddenly the picture began to make sense. 'Is that a lamb?' she breathed, leaning even closer. 'Oh, look, Dad, you can see it moving.'

Fraser Miles smiled. 'Only one lamb there,' he said. 'You can put this ewe in the far pen, Jenny. We'll put the ewes with two or more in the nearer pen, they'll need more feeding.'

Jenny jumped up as her father let the ewe go. 'Come on, Nell, We've got work to do,' she called.

Jenny worked alongside her father and Matt all morning while the sounds of the repairs continued outside. When they stopped for lunch Jenny went out to have another look at how the work was going. The builders had stopped for lunch too but standing in the yard was a stack of roof tiles that hadn't been there before.

'Oh good, they're red,' Jenny remarked. 'Just like the old ones.'

'You wait,' said her father. 'It's going to look just like the old Windy Hill when it's finished.'

Jenny smiled. She couldn't think of anything she wanted more!

Joe Thorburn arrived as they were finishing their sandwiches and he and Fraser had a long conversation about the progress of the repairs.

'I dropped some paperwork off at Thistle Cottage on my way past,' Mr Thorburn said to Fraser. Then he looked at Jenny. 'Anna McLay is there with Mrs Grace. She said she's hoping to have a word with you, Jenny.'

'With me?' Jenny said, puzzled.

Fraser Miles looked at his watch. 'I could take Jenny back,' he said. 'But if you're passing that way, you could drop her off, Joe.'

'But I want to carry on helping,' Jenny protested.

Matt grinned. 'You *have* helped, Jenny,' he said. 'And if Ellen is there, Jess will be there too. He'll be looking for you.'

'OK,' Jenny said. 'But I can come again tomorrow and help with the scanning, can't I?'

'Of course you can,' her father assured her. 'Now go and see what Anna McLay has to say to you.'

Jenny gave Jake and Nell a hug, then got into the passenger seat of Mr Thorburn's van. What on earth could Fiona's mother want to talk to her about?

★ ★ ★

Jess shot out of the front door of Thistle Cottage as Jenny waved goodbye to Mr Thorburn.

'Hello, boy!' Jenny exclaimed as the Border collie jumped up at her. She buried her face in his soft fur and looked over his head at Mrs Grace. The housekeeper was standing in the doorway, looking serious.

'Is anything the matter?' Jenny asked.

Ellen Grace stood aside as Jenny and Jess came in. 'Mrs McLay has something she wants to ask you, Jenny,' she said, leading the way into the living-room. 'But I thought your father was bringing you home and that she would be able to speak to him about it first.'

'Mr Thorburn gave me a lift,' Jenny said. 'What is it?'

Ellen Grace hesitated then she seemed to make up her mind. 'I don't suppose your dad would mind her speaking to you . . .' she said. 'You don't have to agree but Mrs McLay is at the end of her tether. So hear her out, won't you?'

Jenny frowned, but she was already in the living-room and Anna McLay had got up from the sofa and now stood facing her. She looked

26

drawn and very serious.

'What is it, Mrs McLay?' Jenny asked.

Anna McLay took a deep breath. 'It's about Fiona, Jenny,' she said. She looked at Mrs Grace and the housekeeper nodded.

'Go on, Anna,' she said.

Jenny felt a shiver of apprehension. She reached a hand down and Jess licked her fingers. 'How is Fiona?' she asked.

Mrs McLay shook her head. 'She isn't very well at all, Jenny,' she said gently. 'In fact she's been going steadily downhill ever since Jess stopped coming up to Dunraven.'

Ellen Grace looked at Jenny kindly. 'Anna had a word with the doctor,' she put in. 'He said that Jess seemed to have reached Fiona. Somehow, having him at Dunraven seems to help her.'

'What do you mean?' Jenny asked quietly. Her sense of foreboding was beginning to grow.

Anna McLay shook her head. 'I'm not quite sure exactly *how* Jess is helping,' she said. 'Fiona still can't talk about the fire to anyone. In fact she hardly talks at all. She just broods on what she's done. The only time she's been relaxed was when Jess was there. When he stopped coming to Dunraven every day,

Fiona got a lot worse. Dr Scott thinks that her relapse is due to her missing Jess. And seeing Fiona's improvement at having Jess around this morning, I have to agree. She plays with him and it takes her mind off her guilty feelings. Dr Scott thinks that if Fiona can have Jess with her all the time she'll be able to start talking about the fire. If she doesn't do that soon, he says she really will have a serious breakdown.' Mrs McLay paused.

Jenny's heart began to beat very fast. 'All the time . . .' she repeated, putting her hand protectively on Jess's neck. 'What do you want me to do, Mrs McLay?' she asked.

Anna McLay looked pleadingly at Jenny. 'I want to know if you would let Jess come and stay at Dunraven with Fiona until she's better,' she said quietly. 'The doctor is convinced that Jess can help her to come out of her shell. If Fiona goes on the way she's going, she'll have to go into hospital. Jess is Fiona's last chance of getting well at home.'

Jenny drew in her breath sharply and her fingers twisted in the fur at Jess's neck. 'No!' she gasped.

'I know it's a big sacrifice, Jenny,' Mrs McLay went on. 'But won't you think about it?'

Jenny stood up, shoving back her chair. Jess was

at her side, close to her, sensing her distress. 'No!' she said again. 'Jess is *my* dog – not Fiona's. Fiona has never liked him. She made fun of his twisted leg. She called me names. She set fire to Windy Hill. And now she wants to take Jess away from me. It's just another one of her schemes. Don't you see? She only wants Jess because he's mine. Well, she isn't going to get him. He's mine. Do you understand? Mine!'

There was silence. Anna McLay bowed her head. 'Of course I understand, Jenny,' she said, her voice

wavering. 'But I had to try for the sake of my daughter.'

Tears stood in Jenny's eyes and she dashed them away. Then she rushed from the room. 'Come, Jess,' she called. 'Come on, boy!' Good, faithful Jess was at her heels as she ran out of the front door.

She heard Mrs Grace's voice behind her. 'Jenny! Where are you going?'

Jenny ignored her. She was going to the place she always went when she was upset – to Darktarn Keep – and Jess was coming with her. She would *never* be parted from Jess – no matter what anybody said!

3

The wind blew chill as Jenny and Jess made their way across the fields towards Darktarn Keep. Jenny's breath came in great gasps as she hurried towards her refuge. She had always loved Darktarn. Her mother, Sheena Miles, had taken her there often when she was a little girl and had told her stories of the old Border reivers, the sheep rustlers who had raided back and forth across the Scottish–English border, stealing each other's sheep. Jenny nad called Jess after one of the most famous reivers – Jess of Beacon Brae. Now, as she stumbled towards Darktarn, Jenny remembered her mother and the tears slid down her cheeks.

'Mum would never have let them take you away from me, Jess,' she cried, as she laid a hand to steady herself on the drystone wall that stood below the keep.

Jess jumped up on the wall and put his head on Jenny's shoulder. She cuddled him to her as she looked up at the keep. Darktarn was a ruin now but hundreds of years ago it had been a tower stronghold, a place where people went to be safe from their enemies. Just at this moment Jenny felt that she too needed a place to be safe – *and* to keep Jess safe.

The tower's broken, jagged walls stood up black against the sky behind. It looked forbidding in the light of the winter afternoon and the tarn – the little lake below it, looked dark and dangerous. This was where Jenny's mother had died. There had been a storm. Her horse had bolted and Sheena Miles had fallen. But Jenny still loved the place. She always came here when she was upset or worried. Jenny pushed the hair out of her eyes and scrambled over the wall after Jess.

'Come on, boy,' she urged him.

Jenny made for a corner of the wall, which gave protection from the wind. As she huddled there with Jess beside her, Jenny fought against her tears. How could Mrs McLay ask this of her? Didn't she know how important Jess was to her? Jenny wiped a hand across her eyes. And how could Mrs Grace, of all people, expect her to give Jess up to Fiona?

Jess licked Jenny's tears away.

'I'll never let you go, Jess,' Jenny promised. 'Fiona can't really like you. Not after what she's done. Not after all the nasty things she's said about you. She just wants to take you away from me.'

A while later, Jenny looked up at the sky. It would soon be dark and Mrs Grace would be worried about her. 'We'd better go home, Jess,' she said. The word stuck in her throat. Home was Windy Hill, not the tiny cottage that Calum McLay owned.

Jenny decided to go back to Thistle Cottage by the track instead of crossing the fields in the gathering dark. The track led past Dunraven and as Jenny approached the farmhouse she increased her pace. As they passed the gate to the farmhouse Jess suddenly gave a loud bark and scampered under the gate.

'Jess!' Jenny called, but Jess ran on towards the door of the farmhouse.

Jenny put her hand on the gate, then stopped as the door opened and a figure came out into the yard. Jenny hadn't seen Fiona since the day she had confessed to starting the fire. Now she hardly recognised her. At first she thought Fiona had grown taller, then she realised that she only *looked* taller because she was so thin. Jenny's breath stopped in her throat as she took in the girl's changed appearance. Fiona was gaunt, her clothes hanging loosely on her, and her hair looked lank and uncared for. But it was her face that shocked Jenny the most. Fiona's eyes seemed to be huge. There were dark circles under them and her skin was white and drawn. Jenny had never seen anyone look so ill – or so unhappy.

Then Fiona saw Jess and bent down, holding out her arms. At once her face changed, her eyes lit up and she smiled and called out. 'Jess,' she cried. 'Oh, Jess, you've come back to me.'

Jess ran up to her, wagging his tail, licking her face, and Fiona laughed and put her arms round him.

Jenny stood, frozen to the spot, unable to speak.

In a blinding moment, she realised she had been wrong. Fiona *did* love Jess. There was no mistaking her welcome for him. Jenny pushed the gate and Fiona looked up. At once all the pleasure left her face and was replaced by distress. 'Jenny . . .' she faltered, stumbling to her feet. Then she gave a little moan and rushed back into the house, slamming the door behind her.

Jenny stood for a moment, unsure what to do. Fiona clearly didn't want to speak to her. Jess scampered back over to her and butted the side of her leg. Jenny stretched her hand out to him and he gazed up at her. 'Oh, Jess,' she said. 'What are we going to do?'

Although Dunraven was only ten minutes' walk away, it was growing dark by the time Jenny got back to Thistle Cottage. The jeep was parked at the end of the track. Her father and Matt were home. Jenny took a moment to go round to the shed at the side of the cottage where Jake and Nell had their beds. The dogs greeted her affectionately and Jenny patted them.

'Good dogs,' she said, as Jess licked Nell on the nose. Then she turned towards the cottage. She had a big decision to make.

Light spilled out of the front door as she and Jess made their way up the path. Jenny looked at the figures framed in the doorway. Her father was looking anxious and Mrs Grace's eyes were filled with concern. Matt stood behind them, looking serious. Mrs McLay had gone.

'I'm sorry I ran off like that, Mrs Grace,' Jenny apologised.

At once Mrs Grace's face broke into a smile. 'No Jenny, I'm sorry Anna and I upset you so much. I've told your father and Matt what happened.'

'Come in out of the cold and we'll say no more about it,' Fraser Miles said.

Mrs Grace gave Jenny a quick hug and Matt ruffled her hair. 'Don't you worry, Jen,' he said. 'Jess isn't going anywhere.'

Fraser Miles put his arm round Jenny's shoulders as they walked into the cottage. 'How would you like to lend a hand with the scanning again tomorrow?' he asked.

'I'd love to,' Jenny replied. She looked up at her father. 'Will you get all the ewes scanned before the weather turns too bad?'

Fraser Miles nodded. 'Yes, we should finish up tomorrow.' He looked at her seriously. 'Are you sure you're all right?' he asked.

Jenny swallowed hard. She knew what she had to do.

'About Fiona . . .' she began.

Fraser looked down at her. 'We'll say no more about that,' he said gently. 'Anna McLay didn't mean to upset you. It's just that she's beside herself with worry and she's convinced herself that Jess is Fiona's only hope. It's only natural. Your mum would have been just as worried about you. She would have tried anything to make you happy again.'

Jenny took a deep breath, thinking about her mother. Sheena Miles had been the kindest person in the world. She had always thought of everyone else before herself. She would never have refused to help Fiona. Jenny realised that, ever since she had seen Fiona and Jess together she had been working her way towards her decision. 'I was thinking, Dad,' she said. 'If Jess *is* able to help Fiona, I shouldn't stop him. It wouldn't be right. I passed Dunraven on the way back. Fiona came out when she heard Jess barking. I think Mrs McLay is right. I think Fiona really does need Jess.'

Fraser Miles looked seriously at his daughter. 'You mean you're willing to let him go?' he asked.

Jenny nodded. 'But only on condition that if he shows signs of wanting to come home then he should be allowed to.'

Fraser Miles was silent for a long moment, and then he put an arm round Jenny's shoulders. 'I know how hard this is for you, lass,' he said. 'And I'm proud of you. Your mum would be too.'

Jenny swallowed hard. 'It was thinking about Mum that finally made up my mind,' she said. 'And Jess seemed to know Fiona would want to see him. He ran into the yard at Dunraven.'

Fraser Miles shook his head. 'Nothing would surprise me about Jess,' he said, 'He's a very clever dog.'

Jenny nodded. Jess *was* clever. He was also loyal and brave. And Jenny would have to be even braver while Jess was at Dunraven. She was going to be very, very lonely without him, especially with Christmas just around the corner . . .

4

The next day was the day before Christmas Eve – the day Jess was to go to Dunraven. Matt and Fraser Miles had breakfasted before Mrs Grace arrived at Thistle Cottage and had already left for Windy Hill. Another batch of ewes needed to be brought in from the fields for scanning.

Jenny heard the front door open as she popped two slices of bread in the toaster. Mrs Grace came into the kitchen, her cheeks flushed from the brisk half-mile walk from Dunraven. Jess ran to meet her, his tail wagging.

'Dad and Matt have already gone,' Jenny told her. 'Matt promised to pop down and collect me later so that I can help with the sheep. They're hoping to finish today.'

Ellen Grace took off her thick jacket and sat down at the kitchen table while Jenny ate her toast and told her about the building progress at Windy Hill.

'It all sounds like it's coming along nicely,' Mrs Grace said, smiling. She put her hand on Jenny's arm. 'I'll take Jess up to Dunraven with me before lunch, Jenny, if that's OK,' she said.

Jenny nodded. 'I'll get his things ready. He'll feel better having his own basket and feeding bowl with him – and his blanket.'

Mrs Grace looked at her sympathetically. 'Are you sure about this, Jenny?'

Jenny nodded. 'If Jess can help Fiona it would be mean of me not to let him try.'

'You've got a good heart, just like your mother,' Ellen Grace told her. 'I'll bring you lots of news of him,' she added.

Jenny tried to smile but it wasn't a very successful

attempt. Jess trotted up to her and butted her knees with his nose.

'Have I got time to take him for one last walk?' Jenny asked.

Ellen Grace nodded. 'I want to ice the Christmas cake and make up a packed lunch for your father and Matt. You can take it up to Windy Hill when Matt comes to collect you. Give me an hour.'

Jenny watched as Mrs Grace unwrapped the Christmas cake from its tinfoil covering. 'This one won't be up to my usual standard,' she said. 'And I've been so busy, I forgot to get new decorations for it.'

Mrs Grace always made a Christmas cake at the beginning of November but this year it had been destroyed in the fire.

'It'll be yummy,' Jenny assured her. 'Carrie's mum is taking us into Greybridge tomorrow to do some last minute shopping, so I can get some new Christmas cake decorations.'

'That would be marvellous,' Mrs Grace smiled. 'Now, off you go. You and Jess don't have much time left together.'

Jenny nodded. An hour! That was all the time she had left with Jess.

'Come on, boy,' she called to him as she fastened her jacket and pulled on thick woollen gloves. 'Walk time!'

Jess barked excitedly and rushed out of the kitchen door as soon as Jenny opened it. She took a deep breath of the sharp, clean air. There was a stiff breeze blowing off the sea, driving scattered white clouds across the clear blue sky. Jenny looked farther across the water, to beyond Puffin Island. There were darker clouds massed out there. It looked as if there was snow to come.

Jess barked and Jenny whirled round. 'OK, I'm coming, Jess,' Jenny called.

The Border collie loped away from her, turning now and again to see if she was following. Jenny raced after him, taking in great lungfuls of the frosty air. Jess leaped and bounded beside her. In the distance, the sea sparkled in the sun. Jenny laughed as Jess launched himself at her, knocking her over. He licked her face, his tongue warm and rough on her cold cheeks.

'Oh, Jess,' Jenny said, putting her arms round him. 'I'm going to miss you so much.'

Jess darted off, barking at her to follow and Jenny shot to her feet. 'All right, Jess,' she called. 'We might

as well enjoy ourselves. It could be a while before we get to do this again.'

Jenny was so engrossed with Jess that she was late getting back to Thistle Cottage.

'Sorry, Mrs Grace,' she apologised, as she and Jess burst into the kitchen. 'Jess and I were having such a good time I forgot to look at my watch.'

Mrs Grace looked at Jenny's rosy cheeks and bright eyes. 'You two always have a good time together,' she said. 'I'm glad you had a nice walk.'

'It might be the last one for a while,' Jenny said, her eyes losing some of their brightness.

'I know,' Mrs Grace sympathised. 'I know . . .'

'It must be time to go,' Jenny said firmly, guessing what Mrs Grace was going to say next. She had made her decision and there was no turning back. 'I'll get Jess's things.'

Ellen Grace was late and in a hurry, which made packing up Jess's belongings easier for Jenny as she didn't have much time. The hardest part was folding up Jess's old blue blanket and tucking it into his basket. This was the blanket Jenny had wrapped the tiny puppy in when she had brought him into the kitchen at Windy Hill to get warm after his mother rejected him. At that time Jenny had still thought her father meant to put him down because he was small and deformed and wouldn't make a working dog. She had taken Jess up to Darktarn, still wrapped in this blanket. Jenny held it to her cheek for a moment, feeling its familiar softness before she put it into the basket and walked out of the cottage.

'I'll take the car for a change,' Mrs Grace said. 'It'll be easier than carrying all of Jess's stuff.'

Jenny put Jess's basket, packed with everything he would need, in the boot of Mrs Grace's car. Jess trotted behind her, anxious to see where all his things were going. He knew that his basket, blanket and bowl belonged in the kitchen at Thistle Cottage.

'It's all right, Jess,' Jenny said. 'You'll have them back when you get to Dunraven.'

Jess whined and put a paw on her knee. Jenny ruffled the fur at his neck. Then she opened the rear door of the car. 'Up, Jess,' she said. 'In you get.' Jess looked at her, puzzled. 'Up, Jess!' Jenny said again, her voice breaking a little.

Jess heard the note of distress in her voice and stood his ground, refusing to get into the car. Instead, he moved slowly towards her and laid his head against her leg. Jenny bent down and put her arms round his neck. 'You've got to go, Jess,' she whispered. 'I'll miss you and I know you'll miss me, but Fiona needs you.'

Jess licked her cheek and allowed himself to be led towards the car door. Jenny gave him a gentle push and he hopped up on the back seat.

'That was very bravely done, Jenny,' Mrs Grace said as she settled herself behind the wheel of the car.

Jenny smiled a little mistily. 'I don't feel very brave,' she confessed.

47

Mrs Grace gave her a reassuring smile. 'Don't worry about Jess,' she said. 'He'll be well looked after, I'll make sure of that.'

Jenny nodded. 'I'm not worried about that,' she said. 'It's just that this is the first time we've ever been separated.'

Mrs Grace smiled sympathetically. 'You're making a big sacrifice. I'm sure Anna McLay will hugely appreciate your help, and Jess will get extra-special care,' she said softly.

Jenny gave Jess a final kiss on the nose, then she closed the car door and stepped back. Jess jumped up and looked out of the back window as the car pulled out of the yard. Jenny stood there for a long time, looking at the empty track.

Eventually, she turned and went back into the cottage. There was nothing there for her now – no furry companion waiting to play or needing to be fed or walked. Now that Jess had gone, the cottage had lost its last bit of homeliness. It felt strange and empty without him.

Jenny spent the rest of the morning wrapping her Christmas presents. She had bought a thick woolly scarf for her father. Matt was getting a set of colourful cardboard folders to keep his college course notes in and she had bought Matt's girlfriend, Vicky, a CD single she wanted. For Carrie she had got a bright green ski hat just in case Ian *did* teach them to ski when he got back from Canada, and for Ian she had decided to keep a diary of everything that happened while he was away. She would have liked to include photographs but she had lost her camera in the fire. Jenny had found a little silver brooch in a second-hand shop in Greybridge for Mrs Grace. It had been badly tarnished but Jenny had spent a long time cleaning it and now it looked as good as new. Jess's present was the most difficult of all. Jenny hadn't yet found exactly what she wanted and she was hoping she would see the perfect gift on her shopping trip with Carrie.

She looked round the cottage as she worked. Where were they going to put the presents? Fraser Miles and Ellen hadn't had time to think of getting a Christmas tree — but in any case all the tree decorations had been stored in the attic at Windy Hill and had gone up in flames. Jenny sighed. Christmas without a Christmas tree. It just wasn't the same.

Jenny had just finished wrapping her last parcel

when Matt arrived to take her to Windy Hill.

'Ready?' he asked, looking round. 'Has Jess gone already?'

Jenny nodded and Matt ruffled her hair, 'I know you'll miss him, Jen,' he said sympathetically.

Jenny's head came up. 'Maybe I can't have Jess for a while,' she said, 'but I *can* help out with the scanning – so let's go!'

'Good for you,' Matt said, smiling. 'And you can visit Jess whenever you like.'

But Jenny wasn't sure about that. Maybe Fiona wouldn't want her to visit.

The telephone rang that afternoon just as Jenny, Matt and her father got back to the cottage.

'Tim did really well,' Fraser Miles said, walking towards the phone. 'He must have scanned that final batch at an average of eighty an hour.'

'Now all we have to do is get enough feedstuff into the fields before the snow comes,' Matt said.

Jenny smiled at him. 'All?' she said.

'Nobody ever said sheep farming was easy,' Matt joked.

Fraser Miles held the receiver out to Jenny. 'It's Anna McLay,' he said.

'I just had to ring and say how much I appreciate what you've done, Jenny,' Fiona's mother said. 'You've no idea the difference it has made to Fiona already.'

'How is Jess?' Jenny asked.

Anna McLay laughed. 'Oh, he's fine,' she said. 'He seems to have settled in very happily.'

Jenny was silent for a moment. 'So soon?' she said at last.

'He seems to understand that Fiona needs him,' Anna McLay said gently. 'He's a wonderful dog, Jenny.'

'I know,' Jenny said quietly and then, with an effort. 'I'm glad he's helping.' She hesitated. 'Do you think I could come and visit tomorrow, Mrs McLay?'

Anna McLay was silent for a moment. 'I don't know if Fiona is quite ready to see anyone yet, Jenny,' she said.

Jenny swallowed her disappointment. Even one day without seeing Jess seemed a very long time.

Anna McLay was speaking again. 'But I'm sure you could come on Christmas Day – after all, Jess is your dog and Christmas Day is special. I'll warn Fiona and if she doesn't feel up to visitors she can make herself scarce for a while. What do you think?'

'Yes, thanks, Mrs McLay, and happy Christmas.' Jenny tried to sound cheerful.

'And I hope you have a very happy Christmas, Jenny,' Anna McLay replied. 'By the way, Ellen is on her way back and she's bringing a surprise with her. I hope you'll like it.'

'Thanks, Mrs McLay,' Jenny said as she rang off.

So Jess wasn't missing her at all, she thought. She ought to be happy about that but somehow she wasn't.

She was still thinking about Jess when Mrs Grace arrived back. 'Give me a hand with this, Jenny,' she called from the yard.

Jenny went over to the door and opened it. Mrs Grace was heaving something out of the boot of the car.

'A Christmas tree!' Jenny cried excitedly. 'I was wondering where we were going to put the presents.'

'It's just a small one,' Mrs Grace said. 'But then Thistle Cottage is just a small cottage so that's all right.'

'Where did you get it?' asked Jenny.

'From Anna McLay,' Mrs Grace told Jenny. 'She noticed that we didn't have one when she was here yesterday and, when I told her about the tree decorations, she decided that the least she could do was replace them. So now we have a tree and a box of brand-new tree decorations. The cottage is going to be quite festive after all.'

Jenny took an end of the tree and helped Mrs Grace to carry it into the house. Then she went back for the box of tree decorations.

'These are wonderful!' she said, as she opened the box and held up a handful of bright, glittering baubles. Lengths of tinsel followed and a string of tiny white lights. The scent of resin filled the air. Jenny sniffed. 'It smells like Christmas,' she said, her spirits lifting.

Mrs Grace looked at Jenny's gaily-wrapped pile of Christmas presents on the coffee table. 'You've been busy,' she said. 'It *looks* like Christmas too.'

Jenny laughed. Perhaps it wasn't going to be such a sad and lonely Christmas after all. But it would certainly be a strange one without Jess to share it.

5

Jenny jumped out of bed next morning and raced to the window. It was Christmas Eve. She peered out. The sky was heavy with snow clouds but so far it wasn't snowing. Jenny dressed hurriedly and rushed into the kitchen. Mrs Grace had already arrived and was washing up some plates and cups.

'Have Dad and Matt gone out yet?' Jenny asked her.

Ellen Grace nodded. 'They went out early – but

not before I made them a good breakfast. It looks as if we might get snow today.'

Jenny poured herself a glass of orange juice and looked out of the window. 'I hope we don't get cut off,' she said.

'I thought you loved snow,' Mrs Grace said, surprised.

'Not if it means I can't go and see Jess,' she replied. 'Mrs McLay says I can go up to Dunraven tomorrow. How is he, Mrs Grace? Did you see him this morning?'

Ellen Grace dried her hands and reached into her bag. She drew out an envelope and set it down on the table before Jenny. 'This is for you,' she said. 'And don't worry about Jess. He's as bright as a button. He and I had a quick game of tug-of-war with his blanket before I left.'

Jenny laughed. 'Oh, he loves doing that,' she said. 'I wish I'd been there.' She opened the envelope. Inside was a Christmas card – from Fiona. The writing was a little shaky. *Thank you for letting me have Jess*, it said. *I'll look after him, I promise. Merry Christmas, Fiona.*

'I wonder if Fiona plays tug-of-war with him,' Jenny said, suddenly. 'I miss him such a lot.'

Mrs Grace looked at her sympathetically. 'You'll see him tomorrow,' she said. 'And you'll have a nice time out with Carrie today.'

'I'm looking forward to that,' Jenny agreed. 'I feel like haven't seen Carrie for ages. The Turners have been taking their Australian visitors all round the countryside.' She put her head on one side. 'But seeing Jess is different,' she said. 'That's going to be my very best Christmas present.'

Ellen Grace looked at her and laughed. 'You know, with your head tilted like that, you look a lot like Jess.'

Jenny laughed too. 'Now that's what I call a compliment,' she said.

Pam Turner dropped the girls off in Greybridge's busy High Street while she went to find a parking place. The town was bustling with Christmas shoppers. 'We'll meet outside Aston's at two o'clock,' she said.

Carrie nodded, dancing with impatience. 'I've got all my Christmas presents to get,' she wailed as her mother drove off.

'All of them?' exclaimed Jenny, as they made their way through the crowds.

Carrie nodded, her red hair bobbing. 'I just haven't

had time to buy any. We've been driving all over the place. What on earth am I going to get for Mum? And Dad? I can't buy him any more aftershave. He's still got the stuff I bought him last Christmas.'

Jenny took Carrie's arm and dragged her into Aston's. It was the only department store in Greybridge. 'If you can't find it here, Greybridge doesn't have it,' she read as they passed through the swing doors.

'How do you know?' Carrie asked.

Jenny pointed to the sign on the door. 'It says so,' she said. 'Come on!'

While they went round the shop looking for gifts, Jenny told Carrie all about Jess going to Dunraven.

'But that's awful,' Carrie declared. 'Trust Fiona. It's just typical.'

'You know, Carrie, I think she really does like Jess a lot,' Jenny replied.

Carrie snorted but when Jenny told her how she had seen Fiona and Jess together and about the Christmas card her expression became more thoughtful. 'Maybe she has changed after all,' she said. 'She certainly sounds really sick. Imagine feeling that bad at Christmas.'

'Hello, Jenny,' a voice said behind them.

Jenny turned round. It was Marion Stewart. She smiled at Jenny. 'I see you're doing some last minute Christmas shopping too,' she went on. 'You can't have had much time for shopping recently.'

'Hello, Miss Stewart,' Jenny said. 'I'm looking for an extra-special present for Jess.'

'Oh, your dog,' she said. 'He's a sweetie, isn't he?'

Jenny looked curiously at Marion Stewart. She hadn't seemed very fond of Jess when she had met him. Now she was looking around, as if she was searching for someone.

'Did your father bring you into Greybridge?' she asked brightly.

'No,' Jenny replied. 'Carrie's mum did.'

Marion Stewart's face fell. 'Oh, well, then. I must get on,' she said. 'Merry Christmas – and tell your father I'll be in touch.'

'I bet she will,' said Carrie, as Marion Stewart walked away. 'I tell you, Jenny, she's after him.'

Jenny frowned. 'Dad wouldn't be interested in her,' she declared. 'He still misses Mum too much.'

'Whatever you say,' Carrie declared. 'Now I saw some great pottery jugs in the china department. One of those would be perfect for Mum's paint-brushes. Come on, it's this way.' Carrie began to wriggle through the crowds of Christmas shoppers.

Jenny followed her. The shop was so busy that the aisles were crammed with people. The Christmas decorations glittered in the bright shop lights and there were Christmas carols playing over the loudspeakers. Jenny hummed along. 'While shepherds watched their flocks by night,' she said. 'That's my favourite Christmas carol.'

'Why doesn't that surprise me?' Carrie asked, looking innocent.

Jenny laughed. 'Come on,' she said. 'Let's get your jug, then I want to look for something special to take to Jess tomorrow – and I've got to get decorations for the Christmas cake.'

By the time they met Mrs Turner, Carrie was laden with plastic bags and Jenny had found a toy rubber bone with bells inside it for Jess. It was red and green and was called a Jingle Bells Bone. Jenny thought it looked really Christmassy. They squashed themselves and their parcels into the back of Pam Turner's Mini.

'I got a book about the Border reivers for Dad,' Carrie told her mother. 'Do you think he'll like it?'

Mrs Turner looked at her and smiled. 'I'm

sure he will,' she said. 'Did you remember to get wrapping-paper?'

Carrie's hand flew to her mouth. 'Oh, no, I forgot!'

'Just as well I bought plenty them,' Mrs Turner said, laughing. 'Time to go home. I'm exhausted!'

As they were passing the main entrance to Dunraven, Jenny leaned over and tapped Mrs Turner on the shoulder. 'If you let me off here, I can run down the track,' she said.

Pam Turner frowned at the sky. 'It looks as if it's going to snow. Will you be all right?' she asked.

Jenny nodded. 'I go that way all the time,' she said. 'It only takes ten minutes and it isn't dark.'

'Oh, all right then,' Mrs Turner said. 'Merry Christmas, Jenny.'

'Merry Christmas, Jenny,' Carrie said, giving her friend a huge grin.

Jenny clambered out of the car and waved as it disappeared along the Cliffbay road. Merry Christmas, she thought. Would it be a merry Christmas without Jess?

As she turned to walk down the track to the cottage she had an idea. Why couldn't she just take a quick detour to Dunraven and look through the window? It would only take a moment and she might see Jess.

Jenny retraced her steps and pushed open the gate to the farmyard. There was a huge Christmas tree in the corner, its lights already twinkling cosily, although it wasn't yet dark.

Jenny crept across the yard, her eyes on the window. The tree was set slightly back so that she could see inside the living-room. A fire burned brightly in the grate and Fiona was sitting on the hearth-rug with a book in her lap. Her cheeks were faintly flushed from the heat of the fire. But she wasn't reading. There was a smile on her lips and she seemed to be speaking softly to someone. Jenny edged closer still and caught her breath. Jess was lying curled up on the rug beside Fiona, looking up at her. Then Fiona turned back to her book and began reading.

Jenny moved even closer. The Border collie's ears pricked and he looked towards the window. Then, seeing Jenny there, he rose and quietly trotted over. Jenny's eyes pricked with tears as she looked at him through the glass. For a long moment Jess just stayed there, his eyes fixed on hers. He put his head to one side and laid it against the window. Jenny stretched out a hand, then drew it back quickly and stood out of view as she heard a faint voice from inside the room. Fiona was calling to Jess. In a moment she would come to see what he was doing.

Jess gave Jenny one last long look then turned and ran back to Fiona. Jenny caught a quick glimpse of the girl's face as she smiled at the Border collie. There was no doubt about it, Fiona really did love Jess.

Stumbling a little, Jenny turned and slipped quickly back through the gate and on to the track to Thistle Cottage. She had seen Jess, but it hadn't made her as happy as she thought it would. He looked so at home with Fiona. A horrible thought crept into Jenny's mind. Would Jess want to come back to her?

Tears welled up in Jenny's eyes and she dashed them away – but her vision was still blurred. She looked up. Great fat flakes of snow drifted down, blotting out the sky, whirling around her, settling on her hair. The snow had come at last – and it was heavy. Jenny peered at the darkening sky. The snow grew thicker, covering the track, muffling her footsteps, wiping out her footprints as soon as she had made them. Jenny huddled into her jacket and quickened her pace.

★　★　★

Jenny was busying herself decorating the Christmas cake, trying to take her mind off her worries about Jess. She had made a whole scene with skaters and sledges and fir trees. There were even two reindeer and a Father Christmas. It was well after five o'clock before Fraser and Matt returned. A blast of icy air swept though the cottage as the front door opened and they came in, shaking the snow from their heavy jackets. Jenny jumped up and ran to her father.

'Oh, Dad, I'm so glad you didn't get stuck in the snow!' she exclaimed. 'Is it still as bad?'

Fraser Miles pulled off his tweed cap and looked at it. The top was encrusted with snow. 'It doesn't look like stopping for a long time yet, lass,' he said. 'We almost went into the ditch on the track up to the top field at Windy Hill. There's talk of a blizzard on the radio.'

'What about the sheep?' Jenny asked. 'Will they be all right?'

'There isn't anything we can do about them at the moment, Jen,' Matt said, collapsing into an armchair. 'The snow is blowing and piling up under the walls and hedges. We managed to get a fair number down on to lower ground. Let's hope that the snow doesn't get too much worse. We'll try to get up there first thing in the morning. There are bound to be a few ewes needing to be dug out.'

Fraser Miles took off his heavy boots and came to sit by the fire. He looked tired.

'Give me ten minutes and I'll have your meals on the table,' Mrs Grace said. 'It's almost ready. Steak casserole and an apple pie to follow.'

'That sounds great, Ellen,' Matt said, as the housekeeper got up to leave the room. 'We've had a hectic afternoon.'

Jenny looked at her father as he sat slumped in his chair. He had closed his eyes for a moment. He must be exhausted, Jenny thought. She went and sat on the rug at her father's feet. He opened his eyes and rested a hand on her hair.

'Dad,' she said, 'will we be snowed in?'

'If this snow keeps up we might well be,' Fraser Miles said. 'And the work on Windy Hill might be held up until well after Christmas, if this weather continues.'

Jenny sighed. She hadn't thought about that. But it was Jess that was worrying her. If they were cut off she wouldn't be able to go and see Jess tomorrow.

'What do you think, Matt?' Fraser asked.

Matt shook his head. 'You saw the Dunraven track, Dad,' he said. 'If the snow keeps up all night I don't think anything could get through there – not until the snow stops at any rate. It might be as well if Ellen spent the night here.'

'She can have my room,' Fraser said. 'I'll sleep in here with you, Matt.'

'Indeed you won't,' Mrs Grace said, as she came through the door. 'I can sleep on the floor in Jenny's room, if need be.'

'I'll sleep on the floor and you can have my bed, Mrs Grace,' Jenny put in. 'It would be a shame if you got stuck at Dunraven on Christmas Day.'

Ellen Grace smiled. 'We'll work all that out later,' she said. 'Now, who's hungry?'

Fraser and Matt rose at once but Jenny followed them more slowly into the kitchen. Her Christmas Day visit to Jess was looking less and less likely.

Jenny rushed to her bedroom window on Christmas morning. She had slept on a makeshift mattress of cushions and blankets and Mrs Grace had used her bed. The housekeeper was up already. Jenny pulled back the curtains and gasped. The snow must have fallen all night. It lay, white and glistening, right up to the cottage door. The fields around were deep in snow and the track had disappeared. But at least it had stopped and that meant there was still a chance that Jenny could get up to Dunraven to see Jess. Jenny pulled on her dressing-gown and made for the kitchen.

As she opened the kitchen door, Ellen Grace turned to her. The housekeeper was stuffing the turkey. A great heap of potatoes and carrots and broccoli lay on the draining-board, ready to be prepared.

'Merry Christmas!' Ellen Grace called. She had the radio on and a church choir was singing Christmas carols.

'Merry Christmas, Mrs Grace!' Jenny replied, going to look out of the window. 'Oh no, it's started to snow again,' she said.

'Well, we're off,' Matt called, as he and his father looked into the kitchen.

They were both dressed in thick jackets and tweed caps with flaps pulled down over their ears.

'We wouldn't win a fashion contest but we're dressed for the weather,' Fraser Miles joked. 'Merry Christmas, lass.'

Jenny went to hug her father and Matt. 'Don't

get stuck in the snow,' she warned them. 'Not on Christmas Day!'

'We wouldn't dare miss Ellen's Christmas lunch,' Matt said with mock seriousness.

'I should think not,' Ellen Grace smiled. 'One o'clock on the dot,' she said putting the turkey into the oven.

Jenny watched through the window as her father called to the dogs and he and Matt got into the jeep. The wheels spun for a moment, then caught and they were off, chugging up the track. Jenny and Mrs Grace waved, watching anxiously as the vehicle negotiated the narrow track.

Jenny smiled. If the jeep could make it then she would get to see Jess later. She turned to Mrs Grace. 'Well, it's definitely a white Christmas,' she said.

Ellen Grace put an arm round her shoulders. 'The best kind,' she said. 'Now, breakfast for you and then we've got a lunch to prepare.'

As the morning wore on, Jenny got more and more worried. The snow kept falling, blotting out the landscape and piling up against the cottage walls. Jenny kept an anxious eye on the track that was slowly disappearing.

When the phone rang, Ellen Grace went to answer it and Jenny followed her into the hall.

'It's Ian,' Mrs Grace said, smiling. 'They've just got up in Canada. I'll have a few words with him, then I'll put you on, Jenny.'

Jenny brightened up. Ian! He would understand how she felt about Jess. Jenny took the receiver eagerly when Mrs Grace had finished her chat with her nephew.

'Ian,' she cried. 'How are you? Happy Christmas!' When Jenny heard her friend's familiar voice, she couldn't help telling him what was weighing so heavily on her mind. 'Jess has gone to Dunraven to help Fiona get better, so I haven't even seen him today and I'm supposed to be going up there this afternoon but it looks as if we might get snowed in—'

She heard a gasp on the other end of the line. 'What?' said Ian. 'Jess is up at Dunraven – and with Fiona? After all that she's done?'

Jenny explained to Ian about just how ill Fiona had become and the doctor's words of warning and Anna McLay coming to Thistle Cottage to ask her if she would let Jess stay at Dunraven for a while. Ian immediately understood the huge sacrifice

Jenny had made and by the time she put the phone down his sympathetic words had made her feel a lot better.

'You look more cheerful,' Mrs Grace said, as Jenny wandered into the kitchen.

'I feel more cheerful,' Jenny announced. 'Would you like me to lay the table?'

'That would be a help,' Mrs Grace replied. 'There's a freshly ironed tablecloth in the sideboard drawer. And don't forget the crackers and the candles.'

'I won't,' said Jenny brightly, taking a pile of blue and white plates from the kitchen shelf. 'At least we have some of our own things,' she said, looking at the plates that used to stand on the dresser in the kitchen at Windy Hill.

'Yes, I'm glad we managed to salvage those,' Mrs Grace agreed.

Jenny pulled out the drop-leaf table in the living-room and spread the snowy-white tablecloth over it. Then she set to work. Even though they couldn't be at Windy Hill, she was determined to make this Christmas special.

Ten minutes later, Jenny stood back and admired her handiwork. Every plate was carefully aligned, the cutlery sparkled and the glasses shone. Jenny laid a Christmas cracker beside each side plate, then she put a bowl of holly and ivy in the centre of the table between the two tall candles.

Just as the twelve-thirty news came on the radio, the door opened and Matt and Fraser Miles came in, looking like abominable snowmen, and letting in a draught of icy air.

'Something smells good,' Fraser remarked, as he slowly removed his wet coat and hat.

'There are plenty of things that smell good,' corrected his son, grinning. 'I suppose you're going to make us go and get all cleaned up before Christmas lunch, Ellen.'

The housekeeper put her hands on her hips and looked at him severely. 'Indeed I am,' she agreed. 'You're *covered* in snow.'

Matt grinned again and clumped off to get tidied up. Jenny turned to her father.

'How are the sheep, Dad?' she asked.

Fraser Miles ran a hand through his hair. 'We had to dig a few out of drifts but we don't seem to have lost any yet, thank goodness. Getting down the track to the cottage was very difficult. I don't think I'd like to try it again until the snow eases.'

'But that means I won't be able to go and see Jess today!' Jenny exclaimed.

Fraser Miles shook his head. 'I think you're going to have to wait until tomorrow, lass.'

Jenny turned away and looked out of the window at the still falling snow. A lump rose in her throat. She was beginning to regret that she'd ever agreed to let Fiona McLay have Jess.

Half an hour later, they sat down to Christmas lunch. Fraser Miles had lit the candles and now they glowed softly. They had a steaming tureen of homemade Scotch broth to start and then Jenny helped Mrs Grace carry in the main course.

'Wow!' said Matt, looking at the laden table as Jenny set down the big dish of vegetables. 'You really have pulled out all the stops, Ellen.'

The turkey took pride of place. Ellen Grace had set it out on a platter in the centre of the table. There were roast and boiled potatoes, sage and onion stuffing, chipolata sausages, bread sauce, a big bowl of broccoli and carrots and a dish of redcurrant jelly.

'There's Christmas pudding and brandy butter to follow,' Ellen told him. 'Then, if you're still hungry, there are mince pies and Christmas cake.'

Fraser laughed. 'After all that, Ellen, I don't think I'll ever be hungry again.'

Jenny looked round the room. It wasn't home and Jess wasn't here but the little living-room looked cosy and festive. The fire burned brightly in the grate and the lights on the Christmas tree twinkled, glancing off the coloured baubles.

'Let's pull the crackers,' she said, picking up the red and gold cracker from her plate.

Fraser Miles reached across and took the other end of Jenny's cracker. 'Maybe there'll be a lucky

charm in this one,' he said as the cracker popped.

Jenny sorted through the little pile of goodies and unfolded a bright yellow paper hat. She put it on, then exclaimed as she saw what had fallen out of the cracker.

'Oh, look, a horseshoe!' she said, handing it to her father.

Fraser Miles smiled. 'Now that's what I call a good omen,' he said.

Jenny smiled back. She hoped he was right.

Jenny sat back at the end of the meal. 'I'm so full I'll probably never move again,' she announced. 'That was wonderful, Mrs Grace,'

Ellen Grace smiled, pleased. 'We've still got our presents to open,' she reminded Jenny. She turned to Fraser and Matt. 'Jenny insisted on leaving them until you and Matt got home.'

Fraser Miles smiled. 'That was thoughtful of you, lass,' he said. 'Let's open them now, then.'

Jenny got to her feet and knelt down beside the Christmas tree.

'I feel like Father Christmas,' she said, as she picked up the presents one by one and handed them out.

'This one is for you from Matt, Mrs Grace,' she

said, looking at the label. 'And this is for you, Dad, from Mrs Grace.'

Jenny distributed the presents and watched with pleasure as the others opened their gifts from her. Then she looked at her own pile. 'This is so exciting,' she said, unwrapping the first. 'Oh, wow, a camera! Thanks, Dad!'

'There's a film in it already,' her father told her, smiling. 'So you can take some pictures today.'

Jenny smiled and raised the camera, getting all of them into the frame. 'Smile!' she said, pressing the button.

As well as the camera there was a personal stereo from Matt and tapes from Mrs Grace. Vicky had sent a box of scented soaps to her via Matt and Ian had left a gift for his aunt to give her – a book about Border collies with lots of colour photographs. Mrs Grace opened a prettily wrapped gift and exclaimed in pleasure, 'Why, isn't that thoughtful? Look what Fiona has given me.'

Jenny looked at the gift Mrs Grace was holding up. It was a patchwork knitting-bag with pockets for wool and needles. Mrs Grace held it out admiringly. 'Of course, Fiona hasn't managed to get out to the shops so she must have decided to make her Christmas presents. Isn't this pretty?'

Jenny fingered the bag. There were patches of every colour and pattern, all jumbled together, but somehow the pattern worked. 'It's great,' she agreed. 'I didn't know Fiona was good at that kind of thing.'

Fiona had put a lot of work into her present for Mrs Grace, but seeing the bag had made Jenny think of Jess again.

She went to the window. 'It's still snowing,' she said, sighing.

Fraser Miles looked at his daughter. 'I don't think you'll get up to Dunraven today, lass,' he said.

Jenny gazed out at the swirling snowflakes. Jess was only ten minutes' walk away but with the snow falling this heavily, it might as well be miles.

As they sat dozing around the fire, dusk began to fall and the snow continued. Jenny looked at the darkening windows still thinking of Jess. She closed her eyes. If she couldn't have Jess with her on Christmas Day at least she could dream about him. She heard Jess barking. Jenny snuggled deeper into her armchair. But the barking got louder and Jenny shook herself awake. It wasn't a dream. It was real. That really *was* Jess. He was outside in the snow, barking to get in.

6

Jenny jumped up from her chair and rushed to the front door, throwing it open so quickly that it rocked on its hinges.

'Jess!' she yelled.

Behind her she could hear the others, roused from sleep, asking what was going on, but she paid no attention. All her attention was on Jess. Covered in snow, the Border collie hurled himself at her, knocking her over with his enthusiastic greeting, soaking her with his wet coat, licking her face and barking excitedly. Jenny laughed and hugged him tightly, not wanting to let him go ever again.

'Oh, Jess!' she breathed. 'Jess, what on earth are you doing here?'

Jess looked up at her, his eyes adoring, his tail wagging. Jenny laughed again and hugged him tighter.

'Well, well, look who it is,' Mrs Grace cried.

'Not even a blizzard could keep him away from you, Jenny,' Fraser Miles said, bending to give Jess a pat. 'Come on, let's get him dried off.'

Matt laughed. 'He certainly is one determined dog,' he said. 'I'll go and get a towel.'

Mrs Grace shivered and stepped across Jenny and Jess to shut the front door. Snow blew in as she closed it. 'There,' she said. 'Now I think we'd better ring the McLays. They must be wondering what's happened to Jess. They would never have let him out in this weather.'

But just as Mrs Grace was reaching for the telephone, it rang.

'It's Anna McLay,' she announced after listening for a moment. 'Yes,' she said into the receiver, 'Jess is here with Jenny. Why don't you have a word with her?'

Mrs Grace handed the phone to Jenny. 'Anna was worried about Jess,' she explained.

'I'm so glad he's safe,' Mrs McLay said agitatedly when Jenny took the receiver. 'I was so worried when I discovered he had gone. Is he all right?'

'He's perfectly fine,' Jenny reassured Mrs McLay. She looked at Jess. Matt was rubbing him dry with a towel. 'He was so covered in snow that he looked more white than black, but Matt is drying him off now and he'll soon get warm. But we can't understand how he got here. What happened?'

Anna laughed with relief. 'Well, Jenny,' she said. 'Fiona ate a full meal for the first time since the fire. She started to fall asleep afterwards, so I suggested that she should go to bed. Anyway, a little while after Fiona had gone up to her room I felt a draught coming from the kitchen and went to investigate. The door was open and Jess had disappeared. I guessed he might have tried to get back to you, Jenny, but I was worried in case he wouldn't be able to find his way to Thistle Cottage in the thick snow.' Mrs McLay laughed, 'I should have known better.' Then she continued, 'Calum is going to clear the track with the tractor so that Ellen can get back to Dunraven tonight.'

Jenny hesitated, her heart sinking. 'Do you want us to bring Jess back straight away?'

'Not at all,' Anna McLay told her. 'Fiona is still asleep and it would be unkind to bring Jess back just as soon as he's arrived at Thistle Cottage. He must have made such an effort to get there. But I wonder if you would mind bringing him back later this evening? I know Fiona will want to see him when she wakes up.'

Jenny looked at Jess fondly. He would have to go back to Dunraven but not just yet. 'I'll get Dad to bring us up when he takes Mrs Grace back after tea,' she agreed. 'That means Jess and I will have a little time together.'

'Whenever you like, Jenny,' Anna McLay told her. 'I think Jess only waited to see that Fiona was all right before going to find you. He obviously missed you, though he was so good with Fiona I would never have guessed. I can't thank you enough for lending Jess to her.'

Jenny looked at Jess. Matt had finished drying him and the collie came at once to her side. She reached down a hand and stroked his head. 'I'm glad Fiona is so much better,' she said gently to Mrs McLay. 'You must be pleased.'

Anna McLay sighed. 'I'm more exhausted than anything else,' she admitted. 'Fiona has been such a worry to me lately but it looks as if she's getting better at last, thanks to Jess. I'm going to put my feet up and have a snooze now that I know she's sleeping peacefully.'

'That sounds like a good idea,' Jenny said. 'Enjoy your rest.'

'I will,' Mrs McLay promised. 'And I'm glad Jess is with you on Christmas Day, Jenny.'

Jenny smiled. 'It's the best Christmas present I could have,' she declared. 'Merry Christmas, Mrs McLay.'

Jenny put down the phone. Jess was looking up at her, his tail wagging furiously. 'Come on, Jess,' she said. 'I've got a Christmas present for you.'

Jess barked back a greeting and wagged his tail even harder, keeping close to Jenny's side.

'He really has missed you, hasn't he?' Matt remarked, looking at Jess.

Jenny's face lit up. 'I thought he wasn't missing me at all, Matt,' she said. 'Mrs McLay told me he had settled in so well that I thought maybe he'd forgotten about me.'

Matt snorted. 'That'll be the day,' he scoffed.

Jenny led Jess towards the fire and sat down with him in front of the blazing logs. She unwrapped his toy bone and laid it down in front of him. Jess picked it up in his mouth and rolled it over. He looked surprised as the bell inside jingled. Jenny laughed.

'Try it again, Jess,' she said.

Jenny watched happily as Jess played with his new toy.

Fraser Miles looked at the Border collie and smiled. 'He's certainly determined,' he said to his daughter and pointing at Jess. 'That's a dog that doesn't give up. Believe me, that's important in a sheepdog.'

Jenny looked at Jess proudly. He couldn't ever be a working dog himself but her father had once said that his pups would be working dogs – and good ones too!

'Oh, I believe you,' Jenny said, hugging Jess. 'And Jess does too, don't you, boy?'

Jess gave a short bark and snuggled closer to her. Jenny laughed softly. It had turned out to be a wonderful Christmas Day after all. She looked round the little sitting-room. The log fire burned brightly in the hearth, the Christmas tree lights

THE SACRIFICE

twinkled, reflecting in the glass baubles and decorations, and discarded wrapping-paper from their presents made bright splashes of colour. Mrs Grace had put on a tape of Christmas carols, which was playing softly in the background. Matt and Fraser Miles were once again dozing in their chairs.

'Shall I start on the washing-up?' Jenny asked Mrs Grace.

Ellen Grace yawned. 'Later, Jenny,' she said. 'Relax for a bit. Enjoy your time with Jess. I'm going to have a nap.'

Jenny played quietly with Jess as the others dozed. She couldn't imagine a better Christmas afternoon – here with Jess in front of a roaring fire, just the two of them awake. When the phone rang she got up reluctantly and went to answer it. It was Anna McLay again.

'Jenny?' Mrs McLay said, her voice shaking. 'Is Fiona with you? She's disappeared. We can't find her anywhere.'

Jenny gasped. Mrs McLay sounded almost hysterical with fear and worry. 'No, she isn't here,' Jenny replied. 'Why should she be? What's happened?'

'I thought maybe she had gone after Jess.' Anna

McLay said. She sounded close to tears.

'No, Mrs McLay,' Jenny answered. 'She hasn't come here. Did she know Jess was here?'

Anna McLay's voice broke. 'No. I mean, I assumed that she was still asleep and so hadn't been up to tell her where Jess was,' she said. 'But she must have woken up and guessed where Jess had gone and tried to come after him.'

'Mrs McLay,' Jenny said as calmly as she could, 'tell me exactly what's happened.'

Anna McLay took a deep breath. 'After I called you, I dozed off. The others were already asleep,' she began. 'Then, when I woke up, I went upstairs to check on Fiona. She wasn't there and then I looked downstairs and found that her boots and coat were gone from the entrance hall. She must have woken up before the rest of us, discovered Jess was missing and started out after him. I'm frightened, Jenny. Fiona has been so ill. She's still weak. Look at the weather! How long can she survive in that if she gets lost?'

Jenny looked out of the window. Snow swirled against it. 'It's snowing again,' she said.

Mrs McLay's voice cracked. 'It's getting worse all the time. She must be out there somewhere,' she said. 'Out in the snow and the cold. She could be anywhere. We've got to find her, Jenny. We've just got to!'

'We will, Mrs McLay,' Jenny promised. 'Just hang on while I get Dad.'

As Jenny went to wake her father, Jess came to her side, sensing her worry and she laid a hand on his head. The collie licked her hand and Jess rubbed his ears. Despite everything Jess had done for Fiona already, he couldn't help her at the moment. Thinking of Anna McLay, Jenny felt a shiver of fear. She had promised that they would find Fiona – but would they? Would they be able to find her in the blizzard that was raging outside?

7

Fraser Miles got to his feet at once when he opened his eyes and saw Jenny's distraught face. 'What's the matter?' he demanded.

'Fiona is missing,' Jenny explained quickly. 'Her mother is on the phone. Can you talk to her, Dad?'

Fraser brushed past Jenny and swiftly lifted the receiver. Jess was still at Jenny's side. She put a hand down and felt him lick her hand but her eyes were still on her father, speaking urgently into the phone.

'Jen?' Matt said enquiringly. 'What's going on?'

Jenny turned to Matt and Mrs Grace and recounted everything that Anna McLay had told her. Ellen Grace and Matt listened quietly, only occasionally putting a question to her here and there. Their faces grew more and more serious as her story unfolded.

'I wonder if they've called the police,' Jenny said, when she had finished telling them all she knew.

Fraser put down the phone, nodding. 'Anna is phoning the police now but I don't think we can wait for them,' he said. 'Dunraven is only half a mile up the road. The police would have to come all the way from Greybridge – and just look at the weather! It would take them ages to get here. We've got to start searching ourselves.'

'Dad is right, Jenny,' Matt put in. 'And it's Christmas Night. There will only be an emergency officer on duty at Greybridge.'

'I'll help, and Jess will too,' Jenny said immediately.

Fraser Miles smiled. 'We'll all do everything we can. We'll start out straight away.'

Mrs Grace nodded and began to move towards the door. 'I'll get the coats and boots,' she said. 'Matt, you look for the strongest torches we've got, and

Jenny run round and switch on every light in the house. If Fiona is lost out there in the darkness she might see the lights and try to make for them.'

'That's a good idea, Ellen,' Fraser Miles said. 'I'll ring the McLays back and tell them to do the same. It's pitch black out there so any lights should be visible from quite a distance.'

Jenny nodded and rushed to do as Mrs Grace suggested. When she came back, leaving the little house blazing with light, her father was putting the phone down.

'The police are on their way,' he told them. 'The McLays are going to start searching at their end and we'll start from here. With luck we should find Fiona somewhere in between the two houses.'

Jenny nodded. 'That sounds like a good plan,' she said.

'Wait a moment,' Matt said. 'We're assuming that Fiona will follow the track but there's so much snow covering it that she could easily have missed her way and be wandering about the fields. We can't afford to ignore the possibility that she's lost.' He looked out of the window. 'With the snow coming down the way it is, she could quite easily lose her sense of direction.'

Jenny glanced out of the window. Matt was right. The swirling, spinning mass of snowflakes would confuse anyone and Fiona was still weak from her illness.

'You're right, Matt,' Fraser Miles said, as Mrs Grace came in with a pile of coats and scarves. He started to pull on a heavy waxed jacket.

'Where is she most likely to wander off the track?' Matt asked.

'It takes a turn about halfway to Thistle Cottage,' Fraser Miles said. 'The edges are unfenced just there.'

'And there are even narrower tracks leading off the main one,' Ellen Grace put in. 'There are two ways she could go if she missed the track. She could go up towards Darktarn or down towards the cliffs.'

Fraser Miles frowned. 'Either of those could be dangerous,' he said, 'There's the river that runs through the gully below Darktarn Keep. She could fall in.'

'And if she heads for the cliffs she could wander too close to the edge,' Matt agreed. 'It looks as if we'll have to split up. Ellen, maybe you could take the track, Jenny and I'll take the cliffs and Dad could take the Darktarn route. Do we need to leave anyone here in case Fiona turns up?'

Fraser shook his head. 'The house is well lit. It's warm and cosy and, if Fiona arrives here, she'll be perfectly safe. We can do much more good going out looking for her. But I don't want anyone out there on their own. We have to go in twos. It's far too dangerous otherwise. We could end up with someone else lost as well as Fiona.'

'That makes sense,' Mrs Grace agreed, as she pulled on heavy boots. 'But it will mean we have to leave one route unsearched for the moment. We'll have to search the road to Dunraven if only to meet up with the McLays – and we'll have to decide which other direction to take. We can't search three routes.'

Matt nodded. 'Why don't you and Dad take the road to Dunraven and Jenny and I will head for the cliffs?' he suggested.

'Why the cliffs?' Jenny asked.

Matt shrugged. 'I don't know. It's just as likely she's headed off in the Darktarn direction.'

'One thing is sure,' Fraser Miles said, as he headed for the door. 'The longer we hang about here talking about it the longer it'll take us to find Fiona.'

Jenny pulled on her woollen bobble cap and thrust her feet into thick socks before putting on her gumboots. She put on her heaviest coat and wrapped a woolly scarf around her neck. 'I'm ready,' she announced.

The moment they stepped outside the front door Jenny's heart sank. 'We'll never find her in this,' she whispered to Matt.

The wind blew her words away, whipping the snowflakes to a swirling mass that danced wildly in the light from the cottage behind them. Beyond the brightness cast by the lights, the countryside lay in deepest blackness. Even the snow showed up only dimly. The moon was obscured by heavy cloud and fast falling snow blotted out landmarks, making it difficult to gauge distance and direction.

'Keep together, you two,' Fraser Miles called back as he and Mrs Grace set out for Dunraven. 'Look after Jenny, Matt.'

'I will,' Matt called back as Fraser and Mrs Grace disappeared up the track.

Jenny watched her father and the housekeeper go. 'Jess will look after both of us,' she said. Beside her, Jess whined and drew close to her legs. 'Oh, Jess,' Jenny said, rubbing his ears. 'It'll be like looking for a needle in a haystack. Fiona could have wandered anywhere off course.'

Matt put his arm through Jenny's. 'Come on, Jen,' he encouraged her. 'Let's get going!'

'I only hope we've made the right decision.' Jenny told him. 'What if she's gone in the other direction? We'll all miss her.'

'It's a chance we've got to take,' Matt said seriously. 'There isn't any way of knowing for certain which way she might have gone.'

Jess licked Jenny's hand and gave a soft bark. 'Oh, Jess, please help us find Fiona,' Jenny said.

Jess put his head on one side and looked up at her. Jenny gazed back at him, then she had an idea. 'Wait a minute, Matt,' she exclaimed, darting back into the cottage.

'Where are you going?' Matt called after her.

'To get the present Fiona gave Mrs Grace,' Jenny called back She dashed into the living-room and picked up the knitting bag. Then she ran back outside to Matt.

'What on earth do you want that for?' Matt asked, puzzled. 'Come on, Jenny, we're wasting time!'

Jenny looked at him, her eyes eager. 'But this could *save* us time, Matt,' she cried. 'Fiona made this knitting bag for Mrs Grace.'

'So?' said Matt.

'So, it'll have her scent all over it,' Jenny explained eagerly.

'But how is that going to help us?' Matt asked.

'It won't help *us*,' Jenny admitted. 'But it'll help Jess. Jess must know Fiona's scent really well by now. With any luck, he can lead us to her.'

Matt looked doubtful.

'It's worth trying,' Jenny insisted. 'Anything is better than just guessing where she might be.'

'All right,' Matt agreed. 'We'll try it. We might as well.'

He reached behind him and pulled the cottage door closed. Jenny bent down and held out the knitting bag to Jess. 'Find the scent, Jess,' she commanded. 'Find Fiona, please, boy!'

Jess sniffed eagerly at the knitting bag.

'How much did Mrs Grace handle that bag?' Matt asked. 'We don't want Jess finding Ellen instead of Fiona.'

Jenny frowned. 'I hadn't thought of that,' she admitted. 'But Fiona must have handled it much more than Mrs Grace did.' She turned once more to Jess. 'Fiona!' she said softly.

Jess sniffed again then looked up at Jenny. He gave a single short bark then bounded away beyond

the range of the light from the cottage windows. Jenny switched on her torch and located him, just scampering under the wire that bounded the field beyond. Jess turned and barked again at them, this time more sharply.

'What do you think, Matt?' Jenny asked. 'Do you think he's picked up Fiona's scent?'

'He certainly seems keen for us to follow him,' Matt said. 'And that isn't the way Ellen went so he certainly isn't following her.' He suddenly made up his mind. 'Come on, Jen,' he said. 'We've trusted Jess before and he's never let us down yet.'

Jenny raced after Jess, slipping and sliding on the snow beneath her feet. She hoped they could trust Jess this time too. If not, they might not find Fiona in time.

8

Jenny and Matt struggled through the blinding snow. The wind caught the flakes and blew them in great flurries across their path as they tried to catch up with Jess. Their torch beams waved wildly as they lurched across the uneven ground, lighting the huge snowflakes as they fell crazily from the sky. Jenny couldn't see Jess at all now but she knew he was ahead of them somewhere.

'Jess! Where are you, Jess?' she called to him, but

her voice was drowned by the howling wind.

In her eagerness to reach the Border collie, Jenny ploughed on, taking the most direct route across the field. She set her foot down on what she thought was a solid mass of snow but it began to give way. Her foot sank deep into a great trough of snow that covered the ditch at the edge of the field. Jenny lost her balance and put out a hand to the bank that backed on to the ditch. Too late, she realised that it was a snowdrift that had banked itself up against the perimeter fence. Letting out a cry of alarm, Jenny lost her balance completely and unable to stop herself, tumbled into the snowdrift.

At once, the world was blotted out as the soft snow gave way beneath her and closed around her body. Her eyes were tightly shut but she could feel snow begin to fill her mouth as she called out in alarm. She tried to struggle to her feet but it was no good. The more she struggled, the deeper into the drift she seemed to get. She began to panic as she realised that she had no idea which way she was facing. Was she working her way out of the drift or was she digging herself deeper into it? She lashed out, trying to free herself of the clinging, suffocating snow. She couldn't even cry for help. Just as she thought she could stand it no longer, she felt a hand in a thick woollen glove grasp her shoulder and a voice that seemed to come from a long way off, called her name. It took her a moment of confused thought to realise that it was Matt. She grasped the hand that closed over her shoulder, desperate not to lose contact, and felt herself being dragged from the snowdrift. Freezing air and a bitterly cold wind whipped her face as she struggled for breath.

'Are you OK, Jen?' Matt called to her as he worked to free her from the snowdrift.

Jenny clung to him, not wanting to let go, not wanting to be alone again in that dark, cold world beneath the snow. She shook her head and raised her gloved hands to her face, trying to clear her nose and mouth. 'Matt!' she gasped. 'Oh, Matt, it was terrible. I felt as if I was being buried alive.'

Matt put his arms round her and hauled her right out of the snowdrift, hugging her to him. 'It's all right now, Jen,' he reassured her comfortingly. 'I've got you – you're safe.'

Jenny clung to him for a long moment, too glad to feel his arms safely round her to think of anything else.

'Do you think you can get up now?' Matt said

gently. 'It isn't good for either of us to be sitting in the snow like this.'

Jenny managed to get to her knees, still half-buried in the bank of snow. 'I didn't realise I had stepped into a snowdrift,' she told her brother when she got her breath back. 'It looked so solid.'

Matt helped to brush the snow from her clothes. 'Don't let it soak in,' he warned her. 'It would seep through and chill you.'

Jenny nodded and brushed furiously. Then a thought struck her. 'What if something like that happened to Fiona?' she asked, worried. 'You were there to pull me out, Matt. But there wouldn't be anybody to pull Fiona out of a drift like that.' She turned to her brother, her eyes shadowed with worry. 'Oh, Matt. She could be lying in a snowdrift somewhere, suffocating.'

Matt put an arm round Jenny's shoulders. 'Come on.' he said. 'Don't start imagining all the things that might have happened to Fiona.' His words were reassuring but, even as he spoke, he was looking around, his expression worried.

'What is it?' Jenny asked.

Matt frowned. 'I was wondering where Jess had got to,' he said to her. 'He must have heard you call out. It isn't like him to ignore that.'

'Jess!' Jenny gasped. She turned and flashed her torch beam as far as it would reach.

Matt caught her arm. 'Listen, Jen,' he said. 'I heard something just then.'

Jenny listened carefully. She was almost sure she heard a distant bark. Then it came again and there was no mistaking it. It was Jess, and his bark sounded urgent!

'Which way?' Matt demanded. 'The snow makes it really confusing.'

Jenny cupped her hands round her mouth and called Jess's name. The sound of barking came again, answering her call, and Jenny whirled round. 'This way, Matt,' she announced. 'Keep calling him. He'll lead us to wherever he is.'

Calling and following the sound of Jess's barking, Matt and Jenny made their way across the snowy fields, flashing their torches around them as they went, hoping to catch sight of the Border collie. They had reached the field above Dunraven when Jenny stopped for breath. It was hard work, plodding through the deep, uneven snow. She looked around the white landscape as she got her breath back. She could see the lights of Dunraven farmhouse blazing out across the snow-covered fields that surrounded it.

Mrs McLay had obviously taken Ellen Grace's advice. Every light in the place was burning – as well as all the lights in the outbuildings. If Fiona was anywhere around, she couldn't fail to see Dunraven. That meant that either she was lost somewhere out of sight of the farm or she was injured and couldn't make it back to her home. Jenny's heart sank. Then she drew herself up and pushed on. Worrying wouldn't do any good! And where was Jess? Jenny called his name once more and a dark shape flew at her out of the darkness, tail wagging and eyes bright in the gleam of her torch. 'Jess!' Jenny exclaimed, bending down to him.

But Jess was off, racing across the snow to a spot where the drystone wall bordered the top of the field. A huge mound of hard-packed snow, driven by the wind, was piled up against the wall and Jess was perched on top of the mound. He stood there, barking at them, urging them on. Then he leaped over the wall and out of sight. Jenny shone her torch around the area, tested the strength of the pile of snow, then scrambled up the mound on to the top of the drystone wall. She crouched there, directing her torch beam downward on the far side of the wall. The beam illuminated a dark shape lying at the foot of the wall. The shape was half-covered in snow but it wasn't difficult to make out what it was. It was a body.

Jenny gasped. 'Matt, look! Over here!' she called to her brother.

Matt was already pushing through the deep snow towards the wall. He scrambled up and leaned beside Jenny, looking down at the huddled figure below them. 'I think we've found Fiona,' he announced grimly.

Jenny swallowed hard. The dark shape was very still. Matt leaped down from the wall and began to examine the figure that was lying there. The wind had caused the snow to pile up at Jenny's side of the wall so that the ground on the other side was not so deep in snow – but it was very icy. Jenny saw Matt slip several times. He glanced up at her.

'Is it Fiona?' she asked, although she knew it had to be.

Matt nodded. 'She's conscious but only just,' he said. 'It's very icy down here. She must have slipped and hit her head on the wall. The only thing is,

there's no telling how long ago the accident happened.'

'We'll have to get her back to Dunraven as quickly as we can,' Jenny urged, casting a glance towards the illuminated farmhouse below them.

Matt frowned. 'First I'll have to make sure we don't do more harm than good by moving her,' he warned. 'Can you get down here and give me some light, Jenny?'

Jenny nodded and got ready to jump down from the wall. Jess barked a warning and Matt put out a hand. 'Be careful,' he said. 'It's very slippery just under the wall.'

Jenny thrust her torch in her pocket and lowered herself down cautiously. It wasn't hard to see how Fiona had slipped. She saw Matt bend towards the still form lying on the snow and greeted Jess as her pet rushed up to meet her.

'Good boy, Jess,' she congratulated him. 'Clever Jess to find Fiona.'

Jess wagged his tail but his eyes were on Fiona. 'How is she?' Jenny asked as she approached Matt.

'I'll check if there are any bones broken,' he said. 'Can you give me a bit of light with your torch?'

Jenny pulled out her torch and held it steady

while Matt gently tested Fiona's arms and legs. His hands were sure and gentle. Jenny was reminded of the way Matt handled an injured ewe. She looked at her brother's face, intent on his work, and then she shifted her gaze to Fiona's face. Her eyes were closed and her face was nearly as white as the surrounding snow. There was an ugly dark bruise on one temple and a trickle of dried blood ran from under Fiona's anorak hood to her ear. Jenny held her breath as Matt gently pushed back the hood and felt around the wound. As she watched, Fiona's eyes opened and Jenny leaned forward.

'Fiona,' she said gently. 'Don't try to move just yet. Matt and I are here. You're going to be all right.'

Fiona looked at Jenny with puzzlement in her eyes. Then she licked her dry lips and whispered, 'Jess? Where's Jess? He was here but he went away.'

At the sound of Fiona's voice, Jess moved forward and gently nuzzled the injured girl's cheek, licking her face. Fiona raised an arm weakly and tried to stroke him. 'Oh, Jess,' she said, a tear sliding down her cheek. 'You came back. I thought you had deserted me.'

'He came to find us, to show us where you were,' Jenny explained. 'What happened, Fiona?'

Fiona shook her head from side to side. Jenny could see Matt watching her carefully as he worked, checking her limbs for broken bones.

'I don't know,' Fiona said. 'I wanted to find Jess but I slipped and then I don't remember . . . all I remember is that Jess was here again. Then he went away.' She closed her eyes. Another tear escaped from under her lashes and slid down her cold cheek.

'Don't try to talk any more,' Matt advised her. 'We're going to get you home now.'

'But what about Jess?' Fiona asked hoarsely. 'I want Jess. I need him.'

Jenny swallowed hard as Jess thrust his nose into her hand. 'He's here,' she reassured Fiona. 'He won't go away again,'

'Promise?' Fiona said in a broken voice. Her eyes, fixed on Jenny's, were pleading.

'I promise,' Jenny told her. 'Jess is going to stay with you for as long as you need him.'

Fiona sighed deeply and some of the tension went out of her face as she closed her eyes in relief.

'The important thing right now is to get you home as quickly as possible,' Jenny said firmly.

Fiona's eyes opened again and Jenny winced at the pain in them. 'Home?' she said. 'Nobody likes me there. Why should they? I've been so bad to everybody.'

'Jess loves you,' Jenny said softly. 'He found you. He led us to you.'

Fiona sighed. 'Only Jess, only Jess,' she whispered. Her hand went out to touch the Border collie beside her and Jess looked up at Jenny. Jenny couldn't speak – she couldn't imagine what it must be like to be as unhappy as Fiona. But at least Jess had helped her.

'Fiona, you've got to try to stay awake,' Jenny managed to say as Fiona's eyelids drooped once again. 'Fiona!'

The injured girl's eyelids fluttered and then closed again.

Matt frowned. 'That isn't a good sign,' he said, rubbing Fiona's cheeks. Her eyes opened briefly. 'Fiona, we're going to move you. Try not to go to sleep.' Matt looked at Jenny. 'We don't know how long she's been lying out here. There don't seem to be any bones broken but her breathing is very shallow. She could be in the early stages of hypothermia.'

Jenny knew that hypothermia was when a person's body temperature dropped dangerously low – so low that they could die. She pointed down the hill towards the blazing lights of Dunraven in the distance. 'If I take both torches and light the way, can you carry Fiona?'

'Easily,' Matt announced, bending to pick up the injured girl. He stood up with Fiona's limp body in his arms. Jenny looked at Fiona's face. Her eyes were closed and her skin was deathly pale. She hardly seemed to be breathing at all.

'Come on, Jess,' Jenny called to the Border collie. 'Lead the way.' She turned to Matt. 'If we keep close to Jess this time we should avoid the snowdrifts.'

Matt nodded and they set off towards the lights of Dunraven. Jenny crossed her fingers and hoped against hope that Fiona hadn't suffered any lasting damage.

9

Even though they could clearly see Dunraven in front of them, the journey down towards the farmhouse wasn't easy. The snow was deep and Matt was out of breath by the time Jenny guided him on to the track that led to the farmyard.

'You go on ahead and see if anyone's there,' Matt shouted to Jenny over the howling wind.

Jenny nodded and sped off towards the farmhouse. There were tractor marks on the path.

Calum McLay had made a good job of clearing the track. With Jess at her heels, Jenny ran to the door of the farmhouse and rang the bell. There was a flurry of movement, a bark from inside and Paul, his face pale, threw the door open. Toby, his honey-brown Border terrier, was by the little boy's side.

'Jenny!' Paul cried, as Jess and Toby greeted each other. 'Have you found her? Have you found Fiona?'

'Jess found her,' Jenny told him quickly. 'Are your parents here, Paul? Matt is bringing Fiona in now but she needs a doctor.'

Paul peered past Jenny into the swirling darkness. 'They're still out looking for her,' he said. 'Mum wouldn't let me help in case I got lost too.'

Jenny frowned. Then Jess gave a sharp bark and ran to the edge of the farmyard. He stood there, front legs stiff, and nose pointing down the track. Jenny listened carefully. She could hear voices. Then Toby started barking too and ran towards Jess.

'I think that's my dad's voice,' Jenny said.

'Look!' cried Paul. Jenny looked to where the little boy was pointing.

As she peered into the dark, she saw the lights of

torch beams and heard the voices getting louder.

'Jenny!' called Matt. 'We're here – all of us!'

Jenny ran to meet the party coming up the track into the farmyard. Calum McLay was carrying his daughter now. Matt was rubbing his arms gratefully.

Mrs McLay hovered round Fiona, her face anxious. 'Take her straight to the fire, Calum,' she ordered. 'I'll call the doctor right away.'

The McLays hardly noticed Jenny as they hurried into the farmhouse. Anna McLay went at once to the phone and began to speak urgently into it. Jenny turned to Fraser Miles and Ellen Grace and smiled. 'It's lucky you were all just arriving,' she said.

'We met the McLays halfway up the track between Dunraven and the cottage,' Mrs Grace explained.

'Then we caught up with Matt,' Fraser Miles put in. 'I hear we have Jess to thank yet again.'

'Yes – he found Fiona,' Jenny said proudly. 'She had gone looking for him but she slipped and hit her head.'

'How did you know where to start looking?' Fraser asked as they went into the farmhouse.

Jenny explained about the Christmas present that Fiona had made for Mrs Grace as they all crowded into the porch, taking off their wet coats and boots. Jess and Toby came running into the hall, shaking the snow from their coats and soaking everyone. No one told them off; Jess was a hero.

Anna McLay beckoned them into the warmth. 'We've to take Fiona straight to hospital,' she said. 'Doctor Scott says it would take him too long to get here in this weather and, if we can get down the track in the Land Rover, we'll find the main road isn't so bad. It'll be quicker to take her directly to Greybridge.'

'I'll get the Land Rover started,' Calum McLay said. 'You pack whatever Fiona will need, Anna.'

'I'll do that,' said Ellen briskly. 'Anna, you go and sit with Fiona. And Jenny, you go and get warm. You look half frozen – Matt too.'

Jenny and Matt obediently made their way into the sitting-room where a huge log fire was burning. Fiona was lying on the sofa in front of the fire, Paul beside her. Anna McLay went immediately to her daughter. Fiona looked up and said a few words in a weak voice to her mother. Her short dark hair was pushed back from the bruise on her forehead. There was a little colour in her cheeks now. Jess slipped past Jenny and went at once to the sofa, setting himself where the girl could reach out a hand and stroke him. Fiona laid her hand on Jess's head.

Anna McLay knelt beside the sofa and stroked her daughter's hair. She turned to look at Jenny. 'You and Matt have saved Fiona's life. We owe you and your family such a lot, we'll never be able to repay it. All we can do is try and show you in the future how grateful we are.' Tears stood in Mrs McLay's eyes as she finished speaking.

As she got up Jenny went over to her. 'I think Fiona has been very unhappy,' she said softly. 'If there is anything Jess and I can do to help her we'll be glad to do it.'

Anna McLay nodded silently, the tears coursing down her cheeks. Just then Calum McLay came back into the room. As he put an arm round his wife's shoulders, Jenny noticed how haggard he looked. She could hardly bear to watch as he passed a hand over his eyes.

Mrs Grace came into the room carrying a small overnight bag. 'I've brought a warm blanket too,' she said, holding out a pink woollen blanket.

Anna McLay took it from her with a word of thanks while Calum lifted Fiona into his arms. Anna tucked the blanket round Fiona. Then she paused. 'But what about Paul?' she asked.

'I'll be here,' Mrs Grace pointed out.

Paul slipped his hand into Jenny's. 'Will you stay too, Jenny?' he asked.

Jenny looked down at the little boy's upturned face. She liked Paul best out of all the McLays. 'Of course I will, Paul,' she promised him.

Anna McLay made for the door. 'I'll phone as soon as I know what's happening.'

Jenny, Paul and Mrs Grace stood at the door, watching the Land Rover leave. Jenny put her arm round Paul's shoulders and gave him a squeeze.

Matt and Fraser started out to walk back to Thistle Cottage.

'Don't lose your way,' Mrs Grace called after them.

Fraser smiled at her. 'Don't you worry, Ellen,' he said, looking up at the sky. 'Now the snow has stopped it's a beautiful clear night.'

Jenny looked up. She hadn't noticed that it had stopped snowing. She had been too concerned with Paul, and watching the McLays drive off, to notice the dramatic change in the weather. The snow clouds had cleared away and high above them a bright full moon rode in the sky like a silver coin, casting its light over the countryside. Stars studded the blackness of the sky, like tinsel strewn on black velvet.

'It's beautiful,' Jenny breathed.

'Not a cloud in the sky,' Fraser Miles said softly. 'The weather should improve now.'

Jenny turned to him. 'That means you'll have an easier time with the sheep,' she said.

'It means no more snowdrifts for a start,' Fraser replied.

'And we can get up to the higher ground with extra feedstuff,' Matt put in.

Jenny looked once more at the star-studded sky; it was beautiful. She waved to her father and brother as they marched off down the track and then looked down at Paul.

'Come on, Paul,' she said. 'Let's go inside.'

The phone rang just as they were finishing the supper Mrs Grace had prepared for them. The housekeeper handed the phone to Paul, and Jenny watched the little boy's face carefully.

'Mum says she and Dad are going to stay with Fiona tonight,' he told Jenny. Then he listened carefully again. 'Fiona is all right but she has to stay in hospital for . . . what is it, Mum? . . . observation,' he finished, his face puzzled.

'That just means they want to keep an eye on her,' Jenny put in.

Jenny and Mrs Grace looked at each other in relief as Paul finished his call. 'That doesn't sound too bad,' Ellen Grace said.

Jenny nodded. 'Thank goodness,' she said, yawning. 'Oh, I'm so tired.'

The housekeeper smiled. 'No wonder,' she sympathised. 'You've had quite an evening. Why don't you pop up to bed? You're yawning your head off. You may as well sleep in Fiona's room. It's on the right at the top of the stairs.'

Jenny nodded as she smothered another yawn. 'I think I'll do that,' she said. She looked at Jess. 'Goodnight, Jess,' she said, putting her arms round him. 'I'll see you in the morning.'

Jess followed Jenny to the foot of the stairs and watched her until she got to the top. His head was tilted to one side but he wasn't whining. He knew she would be there the next day.

Jenny switched on the bedroom light and looked around. She had never been inside Fiona's room before. It was nicely furnished with pine units, a desk, and a bed with a bright duvet cover. But it wasn't the furniture that caught Jenny's attention. The room was made cosy by the posters stuck on every wall and the books brimming from the bookcases and the tapes strewn across the desk. It wasn't cold or uninviting or empty. It was just like the kind of room that both she and Carrie had. Jenny was surprised. Maybe she would give Fiona another chance and try to get to know her.

Jenny yawned hugely. But right now she was too tired to think. All she wanted to do was sleep.

10

When Jenny woke in the morning, it took her
several moments to realise where she was. She sat
up and looked around the room and the memory
of the previous evening came back to her. She was
at Dunraven, in Fiona McLay's room. She had been
so tired the night before that she had forgotten to
draw the curtains and the room was flooded with
winter sunshine. Outside, the fields were still deeply
covered with snow. In the distance, Jenny could see

the sea sparkling in the sunlight. It was a beautiful morning.

Jenny reached out to open the window a little. Her hand touched a pile of photographs sitting on top of the bookcase and they cascaded to the floor. Jenny bent to pick them up, shuffling them together. Slowly, she riffled through the photos, her forehead creased in concentration.

There were photographs of birds and wild flowers. But there were also photos of people – of Jenny, Ian and Carrie. Jenny had no recollection of Fiona snapping pictures of her. But why would Fiona want to take pictures of them?

A piece of paper fluttered in the breeze from the open window and Jenny put out a hand to stop it blowing to the floor.

Dear Peter, it began. It was a letter. Jenny put it back on the desk. She had no intention of reading Fiona's letter but she couldn't help wondering who Peter was. There was a Christmas card and a few photographs of people Jenny didn't recognise on the desk too. Jenny looked at the card. *Here are my friends. I'm looking forward to seeing the photos of your friends . . . Merry Christmas from Australia, your penfriend, Peter*, the card said.

Jenny frowned. She looked again at the letter Fiona had been writing, wrestling with herself. Should she read it? She had a suspicion now of what Fiona was doing. Jenny reached out a hand and picked up the letter. A few words jumped out at her. *These are my friends . . . I took the photos, that's why I'm not in them.*

Jenny laid the letter down and turned, looking out of the window. The sun was still shining on the snowy, glittering scene below but Jenny's heart felt heavy. She knew now why Fiona had taken those secret photos. She was pretending to her penfriend that Jenny, Carrie and Ian were her friends.

Jenny remembered how angry Fiona had been about the project their class had been set last term. They'd had to draw a map of their house and the surrounding area, then put in paths from their homes to their friends' houses. But there hadn't been any paths marked on Fiona's map.

Jenny frowned. At primary school Fiona's few friends had all been bullies. Since they had moved on to senior school they were in different classes and had drifted apart. Fiona hadn't made any new friends.

Jenny tucked the letter and the photos under a

pile of papers on Fiona's desk. She didn't want the girl to find out that she knew her secret. She shook her head. Fiona must have been so lonely!

Then a thought occurred to her. If Fiona wanted friends so badly, why couldn't she have them?

Jenny and Jess went home that day and the first thing Jenny did was phone Carrie and tell her all the news.

'How was Christmas?' she asked first of all.

Carrie laughed. 'Chaotic,' she said. 'But great. Aunt Babs and Uncle Mike loved the snow. They'd never had a white Christmas before. Mum was really pleased with her jug and Dad is already halfway through his book – and I got some terrific presents. My Australian relatives gave me a portable CD player. I'm dying to show it to you. How did yours go?'

Jenny launched into the story of her Christmas, telling Carrie all about Fiona and Jess.

'Is Fiona going to be all right?' Carrie asked.

'She has to stay in hospital for a few days, but she can have as many visitors as she likes,' Jenny explained.

'I don't suppose Fiona will have many visitors,'

Carrie replied. 'She doesn't have any friends.'

'I want to talk to you about that,' Jenny told Carrie. 'Can you come over?'

'Sure,' said Carrie. 'The snowploughs have been out so the roads are clear. How about this afternoon?'

'Perfect,' said Jenny.

As Jenny put the phone down she nodded her head in satisfaction and rubbed Jess's ears. 'How would you like to go and see Fiona in hospital, Jess?' she asked.

Jess looked at her and wagged his tail.

'That's what I thought you'd say,' she laughed.

When Carrie arrived, Jenny outlined her plan. 'I thought we could go and see her – and we'll take Jess too. Greybridge Hospital allowed us to take him and Toby to see Paul when he was in hospital, so I'm sure they'll let us bring Jess in to see Fiona.'

Carrie looked doubtful. 'Are you sure Fiona will *want* to see us? She's always been so rude to everyone.'

'Only because she felt that no one liked her,' Jenny said slowly. 'Don't you see? She was so afraid of not being liked that she almost *made* people stay away from her. That way she couldn't get hurt.'

'Only she *did* get hurt,' Carrie put in.

Jenny nodded. 'Can you imagine how lonely she must be to have to invent friends?' she asked. She looked challengingly at Carrie. 'Will you come to the hospital?'

Carrie snorted. 'Of course I will,' she said. 'You don't have to ask. And besides . . .' she stopped.

'Besides what?' asked Jenny.

'Well,' said Carrie, tossing her bright red hair back from her face. 'I was thinking that Fiona would only have herself to blame when we turn up. She's the one that's pretending we're her friends. She can't blame us if we make it come true.'

Jenny and Carrie found Fiona propped up in a chair in the day room. She was quiet, and still looked very pale, but her cheeks flushed when she saw Jess. The Border collie ran to her straight away, making a great fuss of her.

'Oh, thank you for bringing Jess,' Fiona breathed as she hugged the sheepdog.

'Is that your dog, Fiona?' a passing nurse asked. 'He's lovely.'

Fiona flushed a little more. 'No, he isn't mine,' she said. 'He belongs to—'

126

THE SACRIFICE

'He's mine,' Jenny interrupted. 'I'm Fiona's friend . . . and so is Jess.'

'Thank you for coming to see me,' Fiona said looking down, 'I didn't think I had any friends.'

'Well, you have now,' said Carrie briskly.

'If you want us, that is,' Jenny said more gently.

Fiona flushed deeply and looked away. 'I don't deserve to have you as a friend, Jenny, not after all I've done to you,' she said.

Jenny laid a hand on her arm. 'Let's forget it, shall we?'

Fiona tried to speak but couldn't. Jess laid his head in her lap.

'There,' said Jenny. 'Jess wants to be your friend too and you can't argue with him.'

Fiona looked up and smiled at last. 'I'd love to be your friend, Jenny,' she said. 'And yours, Carrie.'

'And Ian's,' Carrie said with a grin. 'We come as a job lot. Take one, take all.'

Fiona stroked Jess's nose and smiled more widely. 'I'll take you all, please,' she said firmly.

Jenny looked at Fiona as the girl sat, her hand on Jess's neck and her eyes kind and gentle, looking down at the Border collie. Jenny was glad she had discovered Fiona's secret fantasy about having friends. But she would never tell anyone else about finding that letter and those photographs. Jenny felt sure that, from now on, they would see more of the nicer side of Fiona.

11

It was mid-January now and only a thin covering of snow remained on the fields. The repairs to Windy Hill, which had been halted during the worst of the snow, had restarted nearly two weeks ago and were going better than even Fraser Miles had hoped. It was a Saturday and Carrie had come to see Jenny at Thistle Cottage.

'I'm going to collect Jess today,' Jenny announced. 'Do you want to come, Carrie?'

'Try and stop me,' Carrie grinned. 'Let's go right now! I can't wait to see you two back together again.'

Fiona had been taking Jess for walks since she'd come home from hospital, but now she felt she was well enough to cope on her own, so Jess was coming home – at last!

'I can't wait either,' Jenny sighed. 'Even though we've visited him every day at Dunraven, it hasn't been the same without Jess here.'

'You've been really good about letting Jess go and stay with Fiona while she recovered,' Carrie told Jenny as the phone rang.

Jenny picked up the receiver. 'Ian!' she cried. 'How are you? When are you coming home?'

'I'm fine,' Ian replied. 'And I'm having a great time in Canada.'

Something in Ian's voice made Jenny hesitate. 'I'm glad,' she said slowly.

'In fact I like it so much that I've decided I'm going to stay here,' Ian went on. 'That's why I'm phoning. The new house is terrific and Mum and Dad have missed me a lot. I hope you understand, Jenny.'

Jenny swallowed. 'Of course I do,' she said. 'I mean,

I'm really happy you like it so much – but I'll miss you.'

'I'll miss you all too – and Windy Hill, but I'll come back for visits,' Ian assured her. 'How's Jess?'

Jenny told him that she was about to collect Jess. Then she listened while Ian described his life in Canada. When she put the phone down she looked at Carrie.

'He isn't coming back, is he?' Carrie asked sympathetically.

Jenny shook her head. 'He's really happy to be living with his mum and dad again,' she said. 'It's going to seem so strange without Ian.'

'You've got me and all your other friends,' Carrie comforted her. 'And you'll have Jess back today.'

Jenny smiled. 'That makes up for anything,' she asserted. 'Come on, let's go and get him.'

Dunraven came into sight and Jenny and Carrie quickened their steps. As they turned into the farmyard a black-and-white bundle of energy launched itself at them, wagging his tail and nearly knocking Jenny over in his enthusiasm.

'Jess!' Jenny spluttered, hugging him to her. 'I've come to take you home, did you know that?'

Jenny looked over Jess's head at the girl standing in the yard. Fiona's eyes were brighter than they had been for a long time and she smiled widely. 'I think he *did* know,' she said. 'He's been on the lookout for you all morning.'

Jess transferred his attention to Carrie while Jenny stood up and moved towards Fiona. 'Are you sure you're ready to let him go, Fiona?' she asked.

Fiona nodded. 'I'm sure,' she replied. 'He's your dog and he's missing you. I'm so grateful for the sacrifice you both made, Jenny. Having Jess here was the best thing that happened to me. I don't think I could have recovered without him – or you.'

Jenny put out a hand and laid it on Fiona's arm. 'I'm just glad you're better,' she said.

'I don't really deserve it, but you and Carrie – and Jess of course – have really helped,' Fiona said shyly. 'And today I got some cards – from people at school! I even got a class card. But I guess you two must know about that.'

Jenny nodded, smiling to herself.

Jess ran up and began to run circles round the girls. Fiona laughed. 'Oh, someday I would love a dog like Jess,' she said.

Carrie grinned. 'I don't know about that,' she put in. 'Jess is pretty unique.'

Jenny looked at Fiona as the other girl bent to give Jess a cuddle and say goodbye. There would never be another Jess, but one day Jess would have puppies so maybe Fiona would have a dog like Jess after all. It looked as if Fiona might become a good friend of Jenny's too.

Carrie and Jenny waved goodbye to Fiona and turned out of the farmyard.

'Let's go to Windy Hill,' Carrie suggested.

Jenny agreed. She and Carrie had made several visits to Windy Hill to watch the new lambing barn going up. It was completed now and only needed painting. 'Dad says they should be finished with the inside of the house soon as well,' Jenny said.

Jess ran ahead of them, chasing imaginary rabbits and scampering back to them when they weren't walking fast enough.

As they reached the track that led to Windy Hill, Jenny felt her heart beat a little faster. Jess ran on and the girls quickened their step, running down the last bit of track towards the gate. Jenny pushed it open and walked into the yard. The farmyard was still littered with ladders and paint pots and lengths of wood but the stables looked as if they had never been damaged at all and the new lambing barn gleamed, its fresh paintwork shining in the sun.

'Oh, look, they've painted the lambing barn dark green – just like the last one,' she cried. 'And, look at the house! All the windows have been replaced.'

Jenny feasted her eyes on the old stone farmhouse. The new red tiles on the roof gleamed in the sunshine and the white-painted window frames sparkled. Mr Thorburn came out of the farmhouse at the sound of Jenny's voice and waved to them.

'I've got a surprise for you,' he said, 'Come on in!'

Jenny caught her breath. Mr Thorburn hadn't allowed anyone to go inside the house while the work was going on because he said it was dangerous. She and Carrie followed him into the house. Jenny sniffed. 'It smells so strange,' she said.

'It smells of new wood and fresh paint,' Carrie agreed as they made their way through to the kitchen.

Jenny stopped to look around. The kitchen seemed very bare without the huge dresser that usually stood against the wall, but that had been salvaged from the fire and would soon be back in its old place.

'The Aga is still all right, isn't it?' Jenny asked, walking over to the big black stove.

'It's working perfectly,' Mr Thorburn agreed. 'Now, how would you like to see your room?'

Jenny's heart skipped a beat. The last time she had seen her bedroom it had been gutted by fire, smoke-blackened and ruined. That was almost two months ago now.

She followed Mr Thorburn upstairs and peered round her bedroom door. 'Oh,' she cried. 'This is just how it used to be.'

Joe Thorburn's eyes twinkled. 'I know,' he said. 'I got strict instructions about this room from your dad and Mrs Grace.'

Jenny walked across the room, touching the bright yellow painted walls, running her hand along the white windowsill and admiring the glossy floorboards.

'We had to put a new floor in here,' Mr Thorburn told her. 'The old one wasn't safe any more. How do you like it?'

'I love it,' Jenny answered. 'Thank you so much.'

'You're welcome, lass,' Mr Thorburn said. 'And when you get new furniture in, it'll look even better.'

Jenny smiled happily. 'Oh, I want furniture that's just like the old stuff,' she assured him. 'I want everything to be just the way it used to be.'

'It really will be just like it used to be,' Jenny repeated, as she and Carrie walked up towards Darktarn Keep. 'Except that Ian won't be here, of course.'

'He'll come and visit,' Carrie said. 'He promised.'

'I hope so,' Jenny replied. 'But right now, most of all, I'm looking forward to going home.'

'Home to Windy Hill,' Carrie echoed. 'It sounds good.'

Jenny lifted her face to the clear, cold air. The sky overhead was a pale clean blue. It looked as if it had been newly washed. The winter sun had little warmth but it sparkled on the waves out to sea, turning the water to silver. Above them, birds wheeled and cried and Jenny could see Windy Hill, its red roofs restored, and the walls of the stables repaired. The new lambing barn, bigger than the one that had burned down, stood next to the stable block. Its glossy dark-green paint shone in the sunshine. Windy Hill. Her home – and Jess's.

Jess gave a short bark and Jenny looked round. The Border collie was standing on top of the

drystone wall that ran round the bottom of Darktarn Keep.

'It's OK, Jess,' she called. 'We're coming.'

Jess barked again and disappeared over the wall. In a moment Jenny saw him running like the wind, winnowing his way through the long grass that covered the hill up to the keep. The wind lifted her hair and blew it about her face. Jenny laughed with delight.

'What a perfect day!' she called to Carrie before turning to follow Jess. 'What an absolutely perfect day!'

ORDER FORM

Lucy Daniels

0 340 70438 1	JESS THE BORDER COLLIE 1: *THE ARRIVAL*	£3.99 ❏
0 340 70439 x	JESS THE BORDER COLLIE 2: *THE CHALLENGE*	£3.99 ❏
0 340 70440 3	JESS THE BORDER COLLIE 3: *THE RUNAWAY*	£3.99 ❏
0 340 73595 3	JESS THE BORDER COLLIE 4: *THE BETRAYAL*	£3.99 ❏
0 340 73596 1	JESS THE BORDER COLLIE 5: *THE SACRIFICE*	£3.99 ❏
0 340 73597 x	JESS THE BORDER COLLIE 6: *THE HOMECOMING*	£3.99 ❏

All Hodder Children's books are available at your local bookshop, or can be ordered direct from the publisher. Just tick the titles you would like and complete the details below. Prices and availability are subject to change without prior notice.

Please enclose a cheque or postal order made payable to *Bookpoint Ltd*, and send to: Hodder Children's Books, 39 Milton Park, Abingdon, OXON OX14 4TD, UK.
Email Address: orders@bookpoint.co.uk

If you would prefer to pay by credit card, our call centre team would be delighted to take your order by telephone. Our direct line *01235 400414* (lines open 9.00 am–6.00 pm Monday to Saturday, 24 hour message answering service). Alternatively you can send a fax on *01235 400454*.

TITLE		FIRST NAME		SURNAME	

ADDRESS	
DAYTIME TEL:		POST CODE	

If you would prefer to pay by credit card, please complete:
Please debit my Visa/Access/Diner's Card/American Express (delete as applicable) card no:

Signature .... Expiry Date: ....

If you would NOT like to receive further information on our products please tick the box. ❏